D1760912

The History of Magpies

The History of Magpies

Desmond Hogan

THE LILLIPUT PRESS
DUBLIN

First published 2017 by
THE LILLIPUT PRESS
62–63 Sitric Road, Arbour Hill
Dublin 7, Ireland
www.lilliputpress.ie

ISBN 978 1 84351 666 8

A CIP record for this title is available from
The British Library.

10 9 8 7 6 5 4 3 2 1

Set in 11.5 pt on 13.5 pt Centaur by Marsha Swan
Printed in Spain by GraphyCems

Contents

The History of Magpies

The Big River

The youth, in a tank top that features the alarmingly hirsuted wrestler Deadman, has ruby-orange hair, wears a rosary from Knock, brown as a bog, around his neck, a gold medal of the Blessed Virgin he got from an old woman in a summer dress patterned with yellow Cleopatra butterflies, outside the Bank of Ireland, Castle Street Lower, Tralee.

'I'm from Castleisland on the River Maine but I live now in Saint Martin's Park, Tralee.

I meet up with Travellers – *Mincéir, Misleór* – from London in Knock, County Mayo.

Knock is a beautiful Place.

Our Lady appeared there with a golden rose on her brow.

She was with Saint John and Saint John was reading a book.

I go to the striptease in Tralee.

There's an escort agency with all Polish girls in Killarney and I went out with one of them.'

'Shannon Crotty was my cousin.

He hung himself.

His wife Ethlinn Flavin from Knocknaheeny in Cork hung herself before him.

Her brother Besty hung himself in between them.

A lot of Travellers are hanging themselves now.

One man because he had cancer.

One girl because she was pregnant and didn't want her father to know.

They're all doing it in Finland too.

Shannon and Ethlinn were a bit like Diarmuid and Gráinne.

On the run.'

Diarmuid and Gráinne eloped. If they ate in a place, they didn't sleep in it.

If they slept in a place they'd be up before dawn.

They slept in caves, rocks, under hedges. They hid in rowan trees.

The difference now is that each town Shannon and Ethlinn passed through has a Lidl supermarket and a tableau on the outskirts advertising prospective Neo-Georgian or Neo-Victorian suburban houses.

Because a Catholic priest wouldn't marry them, they tried the Kingdom Hall of the Jehovah Witnesses, Lower Gerald Griffin Street, Limerick, where they briefly received Bible instruction.

After instruction they'd go to Time Out Casino.

It was a bishop of the Palmarian Catholic Church who married them in Belfast.

Click Goggin told Shannon about the Palmarian Catholic Church.

A foxy fellow. A learned fellow.

Used go to Mount Mellary Monastery, County Waterford, a lot.

Started going there when the Blessed Virgin appeared in a grotto at Mellary summer 1985.

Grotto statues of Mary were rocking to and fro all over the south of Ireland then but in Mellary it was an apparition.

The Blessed Virgin appeared to Pope Gregory XVII of the Palmarian Catholic Church, who canonized Christopher Columbus, General Franco, and excommunicated John Paul II, in an Andalusian shrine.

Click had a nostalgia for the Tridentine Mass and that's why he joined the Palmarians who had the Latin rites.

He knew them all.

Johnny Logan. Finbar Furey. Mr Pussy.

Had their addresses.

The wedding party was carried in a British army tank with the crest still on it, sold to man who hired it for weddings.

Some of the members of Slab Murphy's gang from Crossmaglen, County Armagh, attended the reception, one of whom had a tattoo of the comic book High King of Ireland, Slaine Mac Roth, which filled his forearm.

The wedding cake was Chocolate Heaven Cake.

Shannon wore a blue denim suit, black shirt, pale blue velvet tie.

One of his rings featured Saint George of England and another was a half sovereign ring with a naked winged man on a horse.

His hair was a summer saffron.

Ethlinn – chestnut and pineapple strands of hair – had a ring on both hands with word Mum.

She wore a black décolleté top with silver bungle-bead double hem, Naples yellow high heels.

On their way back South they stopped to listen to the Romanian accordionist in black baseball cap with tiny white stars on it, on the bridge of Athlone.

They honeymooned in Mitchelstown, County Cork.

Saint Fanchan of Mitchelstown used to lie, first night of burial in his church grounds, in the same grave as the corpse.

Shannon brought Ethlinn to Kingstown Square to look at the lime trees and the old oak trees.

The Dutch elms had been cut down a few years before because of the disease.

She marvelled at the doors of the signal red, white, Lincoln green, old rose, lemon yellow – Georgian-style and Domestic Renaissance.

When Shannon was a small child (gália, goya) and his father

Hackey and his mother Midna used Ergas, the green bottle, soot used be poured on burning scrap in Mitchelstown.

Shortly after Childermas – Feast of the Holy Innocents – he'd walked into it and his legs were scarred for life.

The couple sat on Nailer's Stone – used by a nail maker once – by Saint Bernard's Well on the oak-shaded Barnane Walk, beside the Blackwater – *Abhainn Mhór* (Big River) – in Fermoy.

A woman tried to build a wall once to prevent people drinking this water but Sir Robert Abercromby took her to court and stopped her.

Travellers would make a pattern – pilgrimage – here as they would to Bartlemy Blessed Well near Fermoy, which sprang from the prayer of a blind man.

Pattern is also the name for the sods of earth put at a crossroads to indicate the direction taken.

The Blackwater Swim as far as the Rapids starts from Barnane Walk in June.

'Three people are taken each year by the Blackwater, and a priest every five years.'

Click Goggin had walked the Blackwater from Fermoy to Youghal once, the cormorants flying up and down and the otter's spraint on the bank, looking for a body that was found the far side of Fermoy Bridge, which has seven arches.

The Blackwater rushes at the ancient spa and casino town of Mallow because it is shallow.

It is deeper, slower at Fermoy, but has treacherous undercurrents.

As Shannon and Ethlinn passed through there were a few rakes of Mallow in baseball caps, throwing rocks at passersby on Ten Arches Bridge, Mallow, from the Bull Works, one three-quarters immersed in the Blackwater in a scarlet T-shirt that said Enjoy Cocaine.

Shannon had had a run in with a bouncer in a north Kerry resort where some of the Limerick boys carry shot guns, was handcuffed, escaped, the handcuffs lost and never recovered, this being one of the main contentions, but it was his brother Bradley – who drove a chipwagon to occasions like the Lammas Fair in Ballycastle, County Antrim, which commences with a procession of mourners for the golden-haired Lug – God of fertility – who carry hooped wreathes – who was blamed.

The same gingerbread-coloured hair – a shade from the old red sandstone of the Galtee Mountains.

Bradley was called back from as far afield as Achill Sound for court appearances.

Courtroom wardrobe in peach and beige court rooms – oiled wideleg trousers, filthy trackies, track suit bottoms with cheeks of buttocks prominently on view, predominant black and white in track suits, which was probably why there were so many panda in brothel jokes during the rounds.

Contraband mobile phone are clenched between buttocks now and thus snuggled into prison cells.

These prisoners are like hotels: you can choose your cell but you can't wash your teeth in them.

When the Guards – *séids*, bluebottles – realized their mistake they didn't apologize.

'You have until six,' they tell Travellers at halting sites now.

Weren't the Gypsies sent to Auschwitz?

In their trailer the newly weds had a picture of two elephants kissing, horns wrapped around one another's trunks: a photograph of Santa Claus presenting a cup for hurling to Shannon as a child, in a black bow tie; the dead Hunger Striker Martin Hurson with miner's locks, white shirt, white tie, smile reserved for weddings; a statue of Saint Patrick with ashen hair and peach lips; a parrot with flaked red head; a pair of beige polka-dot wellingtons; a donkey and four Edwardian children, boy in young Edward VIII cap, clinging to a little girl's waist on top of the donkey.

Although neither could read they had a copy of *Black Beauty* by Anna Sewell with Black Beauty on the cover with white star on his forehead, three-penny bit of white hair on his back, rook's wing coat, one white foot: Click Goggin had not only given it to them as a wedding present but had read it to them in instalments so they knew of the blackberry-addicted ploughboys; the river-consumed toll-bridges; the shaggy midget Welsh ponies at horse fairs; the long black funeral coaches covered with black cloth and drawn by black horses.

A house near the town was converted into an FCA barracks during the Emergency (War years) and roughness was attributed to this.

In the Sorrento Café you could have gravy chips and a strawberry milkshake.

It was common to see a Traveller youth in a hoodie jacket being harassed outside, beside his Honda Cub 90 motorbike, by a garda.

The nightclub where a girl did a pole dance – entwined herself to a chrome pole – if you gave her money, was beside the graveyard.

Hiring fairs used be held here …

'Buy marking stones.

I've marking stones of colour red.'

Rabbits brought in on the crossbars of bicycles.

Tame blackbirds sang the airs of ballads like Carrickfergus.

'I would swim over … the

deepest ocean for

my love to find.'

There was a hotel known as the Murderer Doody's Hotel.

Doody and his wife had been alcoholics and he'd murdered her and was put in the Criminal Asylum in Dublin.

The bells and whistles of a funfair were heard at the beginning of the summer, disturbing the flaming-sienna skewbald horses, but now war-helicopters were featured in the fairground iconostasis alongside the men in Batman masks and women with immense breasts with cross-thonged décolletage.

Shannon and Ethlinn always listened to Country Sound in Mallow on Sunday nights; Peter Burke, Johnny Barrett, Charlie Coughlin, Gillian Welch, Johnny Cash and his brother Tommy Cash, Dickie Rock's son Richie Rock.

Ethlinn's favourite singer was the keen-featured Lacy J. Dalton from Bloomsburg Pennsylvania who'd drifted around the United States as a girl, her husband victim of swimming tragedy.

Shannon's favourite singers were Charlie and Ira Louvin from the Southern Appalachians – fifties toyboy grins, squared off ties, the first a Korean War veteran, the second doomed to die in a Missouri car crash with three bullets permanently lodged in his spine, a presentation from an outraged wife: who sang of trains, blind-drunkenness, of the River Jordan that, to the accompaniment of a mandolin and rockabilly guitar, called these things into its current.

Shannon's parents, whose marriage had been arranged by the Traveller matchmaker Cowboy McDonagh up in Galway, used go to Maudie Mac's hostelry in Newtwopothouse near Mallow to hear Gina Dale Hayes and the Champions, T.R. Dallas, Big Tom and the Mainliners.

In their brief married life Shannon and Ethlinn would attend the Buttevant Horse Fair on 12 July at Cahirmee Field, where Shannon had seen the Traveller singer Margaret Barry arrive on a bicycle with a banjo slung over her shoulder.

After the Fair they'd go to the Park, Doneraile to have a swim in the Awbeg River, bringing refreshments of Club Orange and Super Milk Shakes – very fluffy pink marshmallows.

In Doneraile there is a takeaway called Night Bites.

The young people who gathered around it at night started terrorizing a man who lived by himself opposite it, urinating through his letter box.

The man drowned himself in the Awbeg.

Sometimes Shannon would throw a rope with a net over it over the Awbeg at Castletownroche, which joins up with the Blackwater a few miles on, to catch trout and when the *séids* would come he'd say he was drying clothes.

You'd often see Shannon driving a sulky up and down, past the ball alley, on Island Field in Limerick, swans in the turloughs (winter lakes), the Island – the entrance to which is guarded by two phoe-nixes facing one another – pointillist with the amount of garbage stomped into the ground, the greensward so full of horses it looked like the Wild West.

His scarlet and yellow sulky, festooned with white ribbon, was drawn by an Italian skewbald with a face like Sylvester Stallone.

Shannon would wash that horse's hooves with Superway Car Oil.

The boys from Donogh O'Malley Park in Limerick would break into funeral cars parked outside Mount Saint Oliver Cemetery and rob them.

It was common to find a funeral car torched against a lamppost at the beginning of Raheen Industrial Estate.

'I don't judge them,' Shannon would say.

He had a barleywater and white greyhound (yelper), a magpie grey-hound, two miniature Jack Russells and six Patterdales – dark terriers with markings like the Milky Way.

Patterdales take their name from a locale in the English Lake District and were used to combat the grey, greyhound-build, wolfish fox of the Lake District.

He also had three blue-grey and ten Yorkshire terriers that, to the wagers of miners, used kill rats in matches between pairs of them to see which would destroy the most rats in the shortest time.

The greyhounds and the terriers were kept in separate cages alongside the trailer because the greyhounds would destroy the terriers if they got a chance.

The terriers were used to turn foxes from their earths and badgers from their setts.

Shannon also had a gun to shoot foxes.

He used shoot pheasants by the Blackwater with it too.

On a pilgrimage to the monastery of Clonmacnoise on its found-er's, Saint Ciaran's Day, 9 September, Shannon had got a bracelet of tiny ikons: Our Lady of Medjugorje holding Infant as on her first appearance June 1981, never again, in the many apparitions, seen with the Infant; cropped haired, edgy-featured Pier Georgio Frassati, the skiing saint, a sexy saint, who as he died of polio at twenty-four in Turin scribbled a message with paralyzed hand reminding a friend not to forget the injections for Converso, a poor man; the geranium-mouthed mulatto Saint Martin de Porres, first black saint of the Americas, who opened a shelter for stray cats and dogs in Lima and cared for poor farmhands, black people, mulattoes; Saint Catherine Laboure in her breath-taking wimple of the Daughters of Charity, with rings on her fingers like a Traveller girl, with whom Our Lady sat on a chair at 140 Rue du Bac, Paris, had a chat with her and gave her the oval Miraculous Medal.

'A holy yoke,' Shannon called the bracelet.

He'd put raffia in the soffit of eaves and put in PVC windows with a friend, Lippo Taaffe.

Lippo had a cobalt rosary from Medjugorje around his neck, tattoo of a carp amid a garden of oriental flowers on his right forearm, miscellaneous Celtic tattoos – the work of a tattooist in Belfast – on his right buttock.

He was put in Porlaoise Jail.

He put his wedding ring in his leopard-print shoe and it smashed to pieces.

His wife threw her wedding ring over a shed and that was the end of the marriage despite the fact she'd taken three marriage courses in Limerick.

She had Lippo's child who tore at her hair.

Judas hung himself on the elder tree. Christ was crucified on the elder tree.

Ethlinn hung herself on an alder tree by the Blackwater.

The common alder had matted orange roots that form dense mats and these slow down the erosion of the Blackwater banks.

Irish mahogany the wood from the common alder is called, because of its bloody colour.

The trout, who carry newly born mussels upstream in their gills at this time of year – the mussel may live for one hundred and thirty years – consume earwigs, Mayflies, stoneflies that surround the early summer alders.

Liam Ó Maonlaí of Hothouse Flowers, who won the All Ireland final as bódhran – Irish tambourine – player when he was seventeen, was singing in town the night Ethlinn hung herself, beside the Murderer Doody's Hotel.

'The war being over, and he not returned . . .
Dear Irish Boy . . . *An Buachaill Díleas*.'

Her parents wanted Ethlinn to be buried in Cork.

Shannon wanted her buried by the Blackwater.

As appeasement she was buried in neither place but a town where once a Spanish nobleman of immense wealth came after murdering his Genoese son-in-law for marrying his daughter against his wishes, retiring into a Chapter Room of the Franciscan Friary out of remorse, surviving on a diet of bread and water, dying there, and buried by the Cloisters; where there used be a Lazaret – a treatment centre for Lepers – and to this day there's a pond called The Leper's Pond – *Loch an Lobhar.*

The raven pairs for life. The mute swan and its partner build an enormous reed nest for themselves. A starling couple make a nest in a rabbit hole with moss and song-thrush feathers. But Shannon and Ethlinn's marriage kamikazed after three years.

'You can't get up from the grave and go to the shop for ten cigarettes. You never see a trailer on a hearse,' a Traveller with a Grim Reaper tattoo on his arm was heard to say at the funeral.

The Crottys came in the night and erected a colossal cast-concrete headstone on which rockabilly guitars were carved.

A mistle-thrush sang on the headstone thereafter.

Ethlinn's brother Besty committed suicide in Kilbarry in Cork later that summer, also by hanging, in his case in the house, an ephebe at Collins Barracks, Cork, in burgundy beret, the colour of St John's Wort or bird's foot trefoil in his face.

'It's because of depression,' a man with a tattoo of a reclining lion cub, was heard to say at the funeral.

'Because they all slept together in Knocknaheeny,' a man with a tattoo of a cross composed of two hands in prayer at the bottom, an eye at each side, a rosary wound about the top, said to a youth in a black Samurai suit patterned with gold dollar signs, as they walked away,' they used break in ten-year-old boys like Besty.

And then when the ten-year-old boys were fifteen they'd break in others.

And the dolls.'

They were followed by a Traveller girl with honey-colour pancake makeup, in a low-cut black dress with silver-work squares and discs.

It was a wet summer.

Noah made his Arc of gopher wood.

No man knows what gopher wood is but the assumption is that it was cypress, gopher and cypress similar in Hebrew.

American yellowwood, which has white blossoms, is known as gopher but it was not Noah's tree.

Butterbur, the large soft leaves of which were once used to wrap butter, was growing by the Blackwater when Ethlinn committed suicide: glasswort, its viridian spikes once burned for glass-making, was growing by the Blackwater when Shannon committed suicide, hanging himself on the common alder.

Tásped – dead.

Barnane Walk was carpeted with beech nuts the squirrels feed on and pine nuts the pigeons partly chew.

Queen Victoria once came to the Blackwater in Fermoy to review her troops.

Black crepe had hung on every single door in Fermoy after the Munster Fusilier casualties at Sedd el Bahr on the Gallipoli Peninsula August 1915.

Lug of the golden hair dies at Lammas – 1 August – and is born again with Bealtaine – 1 May.

Kings of Ireland were given lordship of the earth for a year and a day and then sacrificed on it, their veins opened onto it.

They buried Shannon in a cemetery like ashes on a hill under a church with Gothic spire.

'But the sea is wide
and I cannot swim
over ...'

The Traveller Finbar Furey, who keened the Munster Fusiliers of Gallipoli, Liam Ó Maonlaí, and a blackbird at the fair had sung that song.

Shannon and Ethlinn's son Ryan is a nestling-robin child with lapis lazuli eyes.

The young herons croak and clap their beaks in the tall trees by the Blackwater – the *Abhainn Mhór* – January to June.

Now they have companions because the snow white little ogrets have come and built their nests in the tall Blackwater-side trees among the herons, mostly in the tidal area, but some here too.

Ryan Crotty stands by a field of herons with two little egrets among them.

Garach na Glóire they call the loosestrife by the river – Obliging the Glory, or *créachtach* – wounded.

The young cuckoo knows how to make its own way back to Africa in July or August after its parents, which abandoned it, have gone ahead.

Ryan Crotty knows how to talk to a stranger.

'You knew Shannon.

Shannon was my Daddy.

Shannon is dead.'

Café Remember

'You'll never fit in here,' an Irish woman told me on a street in West London — still war-time colours: teal-blues, Santa-Claus reds, mushy-pea greens.

An advertisement for Summer County Margarine on the street that showed a Home County dingle.

A shaven-headed youth stood on the street under a lamppost like a liquorice twister, in a vertically striped polo shirt with blue collar that had a white- and scarlet-lined hem, who could have been one of those Spitalsfield youths tucked in a corner of a Gilbert and George photo montage.

About a year later I had tea from a mug with a monk's face and a slice of double chocolate cake in that woman's small flat.

A photograph on the cabinet of a girl in black stretch tights, with a strap under the instep, ski-fashion, and early sixties eye make-up outside a country cottage with flowering redcurrant alongside it, beside a picture of youths with alpenstocks with the words: 'A Swiss Scene,' under it, and a lustre jug.

A black woman, in a jacket with a deep flared peplum, walks, head in the air, with a bunch of salmon-coloured carnations, by Champion Park Station.

A youth with an understated sleeper and Battleship Potemkin beret darts among the young homeless close to Victoria Station.

'Why are you wearing the beret? Are you in the Foreign Legion?'

'Paddy's Wagon they call the Cathedral,' a youth in a jacket the drab-blue of summer days in Scarborough, tells me.

'Liverpool was born when the Irish went there. Liverpool team was born in 1891 but it wasn't really born until 1892 because it shared grounds with Everton.

In 1892 Liverpool got its own grounds and Everton got its grounds.

I want to go home. Tarbuck Road.

Hoyton.'

A youth in a roll neck grey-white jersey, central band with black line running through it, immediately follows on from him.

'Bird's gone off with me mate. She's from Birmingham. I'm from Wales. I don't speak Welsh. Rhonda Valley and all that. I've been here too long.

The Roman soldiers marched to the Isle of Anglesea, wiped out the oak groves.

I stay with me mates and lie on the floor with them.

I don't want to go to a hostel.'

The graffiti says:

'Don't be afraid to be weak.

Look in your heart, my friend.

There you will find yourself.

The return to innocence.'

A youth in a wine jersey apologized for by a string of beads or two, who has recently got out of HMP Gartree, Wakefield, sings a gung-ho version of Shane MacGowan's 'A Rainy Night in Soho.'

On the boat to Ostend an old bearded Jewish man in a hat, prayer shawl – tallow and black striped – leans over a cafeteria table, quietly droning prayers.

In Antwerp Central Station there is a fanfare of yellow embossments on the cafeteria wall. The chandeliers are gold cylinders. Nuns in oyster grey slouch by and the men's lavatory is filled with mimosa and gypsophilia, and is tended by a woman in a pinafore flowered with what looks like Virginian cowslips – blue cowslips.

At the cafeteria counter a youth in a beige jersey carded with London smells leans toward me as if to say something.

River Phoenix – blow-dried cockscomb and backwoods lumber-jackets – dies; Caroline Kennedy Schlossberg, with Hippolyte, Amazon queen pompadour, kisses Jacqueline Lee Bouvier's coffin in Arlington National Cemetery, Virginia, watched by restrained magnifico girls in black; Kurt Cobain of Nirvana, who had a tattoo from Amsterdam's Hanky Panky – Henk Schiffmacher – shoots himself; Alexandr Solzhenitsyn returns to the Gulag with his blond and wondering son; Gerrit van Honthorst's (Gherardo delle Notti) – whose portrait of herself Maria de' Medici, Queen of France, presented to the City of Amsterdam which still has it – *Nativity*, is destroyed by a bomb at the Uffizi in Florence – a torn, ochre canvas all that's left of it; a drawing by Carlo Maratta – who placed his Madonna among traffic jams of angels – of Madonna and Child in pen and brown ink and wash over black chalk turns up after three centuries pinned to the kitchen door in a Birmingham council house.

The coot – black head, red eye, white frontal shield – lives on Amsterdam harbour as it does on the slow rivers of Ireland.

You can hear the sharp and lonely cry of the coot, like branches breaking, here too.

The trimming of Amsterdam across from Stationsplein – lime trees, plane trees.

A man in a sea captain's cap, blows a gold horn that had been hanging around his neck, by the Amstel River to announce the departure of a boat.

On the wall of a Jewish café is a black and white photograph of an old Jewish lady giving chrysanthemums to Princess Juliana on

9 September 1938 in the Jewish Invalid Hospital.

Prince Bernard always wore a white carnation an old Jewish lady in a sweater with two appliqué birds on it, a wheelchair beside her table, tells me, and this was adopted as a symbol by the Dutch Resistance.

George Hendrik Breitner who sketched the poorer area of The Hague with Vincent van Gogh, who found his pregnant prostitute Sien there, painted the white carnations – *anjelieren* – of Holland – nervous creatures.

The streets of Amsterdam are like the moss-hung plantation oaks of Louisiana.

Descartes, whose entire philosophical vision came to him in a dream during the Thirty Years War and who was to die of cold in the court of Queen Christina of Sweden, wrote to Guez de Babac that he went out walking in the confusion of the Amsterdam crowds with as much tranquillity as he would in his own garden paths.

Above doorways on houses with step gables, bell gables, Italian gables are a black ram: a small vessel on a sea of nervous waves; a rowan tree in berry; a Moor in dog-rose garb; a mermaid; a quarter moon.

Packed flotsam in bar and café windows: action men – regular soldiers and mercenaries from all over the globe; Droste's cocoa tins – burnt orange; '*Je ne fume que le Nils*' – a Scheherazade in lavender robes and raffia sandals smoking a cigar under a Nile-side palm tree; two ornamental swans hem in a miniature table with Turkish weaving on it, yellow, orange and olive flowers on purple.

Rembrandt spent his life collecting stage props, which he placed alongside the models in his paintings.

Years ago I knew a girl from Galway City who came to Amsterdam and had a flat on Oudezijdsacterburgwal, near Café Remember.

I met her in the café once, under a reproduction of Rembrandt's *Rape of Ganymede* – a *somachán* (plump youngster), a bawling Dutch Ganymede, brick-coloured hair, bottom about to be raped shaped like a goldfish bowl.

She was wearing a black dress with a galaxy of all-white oriental trees in blossom on it, a brimless knitted beret, and she spoke of the Claddagh in Galway City: *Cladach* – site of an ancient shore-side fishing community.

I was with a girl who had lemon-yellow hair, a Grecian nose, and was wearing a green blouse with cup sleeves, which had a Mickey-Mouse pattern.

The girl from Galway City died in Amsterdam some months later of a heroin overdose.

A girl in a dress with a pattern of ladies with Hedy Lamarr in sombreros, with hoop earrings, holding bunches of calla lilies or single peach roses, motif of conquistadorial Mexican churches and cactuses, cycles by.

A Romanian youth plays an accordion with the blue, yellow and red of Romania on it: a coat of arms eagle; a pelican of the Danube delta; a sunshade congested Black Sea resort; the exterior of a church covered with religious paintings like a body with tattoos.

On Johnny Jordan Square an old Ashkenazi Jewish man smokes a pipe with a fist carved at the end of it, contre-jour against Prinsengracht Canal.

Above Prinsengracht Canal is Westerkerk, the largest Protestant church in the Netherlands, which has the aquamarine crown of Maxmilian of Austria on top who gave the City of Amsterdam the right to use imperial arms in 1489 after a pilgrimage he made to the city.

'Volumes that I prize above my dukedom.'

Books define leaving, define departure.

In a time of terror slim volumes are what survive, are what's transportable. Your books crossing the Irish Sea.

Walking along a road in south-east London, Irinia Ratushinskaya's cloudy face exposed from a cover.

The books, the grand number of them, are whittled down until there are only a few Russian faces, faces of people who have been in prison, or have queued outside prisons for news of those close to them.

'Beg from a beggar and you'll never be rich.

Beg from a beggar and you'll end up in the ditch.'

The beauty of the town I came from: a row of town houses of kingfisher orange.

The trees that were at the end of the street: oak trees, the sweet chestnut, the horse chestnut.

The river.

In my father's youth, during the Second World War, there was a woman who lived in a London brick orange house near the river who would sing Gounod's 'Oh That We Two Were Maying' at rugby parties.

'God bless De Valera and Seán MacEntee.

They gave us the black bread and an ounce of tea.'

Mrs Mulloy, who lived in one of those houses of kingfisher orange, bought a Christmas gift for you one year.

You were summoned across the street to receive it. She was waiting for you at the door in a cardigan under a framed poem by Rachel Arbuckle:

'May the road rise to meet you ...'

The gift was the *Ladybird Book of Nature*, which told you about the kitten caterpillar and the dahlia anemone.

You transcribed the information in a plum-covered Ormond exercise book.

Perhaps because it was coming near D-Day anniversary – they were nights of low tide, bright moonlight on the English Channel but on June fifth there was a storm so the chosen night was the sixth, Gold, Sword, June the British naming beaches, Omaha, Utah, the names Americans choosing for their beaches – in the William IV box-shape house where I'd had a flat for twelve years, my landlady, in forties-style frilled short-sleeved top and red linen skirt, on a chair with lion paws at the end of the legs, under a painting of Alexander the Great in India on a horse with a cheek-rosette and collar with hanging plaques, took out family photographs.

The older boys with crinkled hair – marcel waves.

'Friday night is Amami night,' went the slogan for the brand of shampoo.

The boys in white shirts with sleeves in fouclé rolls, by winkle stalls on seaside piers, eating crab sandwiches or biting seaside rock.

In bathing costumes of jersey wool from shoulders to upper thigh.

Bombing raid nights they used spend in the Lewisham Odeon – there were interludes on the organ, sing-songs, amateur talent shows.

They'd even dance the Slap-Bum polka as London was being bombed.

The Cider House, Lupus Street, Pimlico, kept going during the War: Gin and Cider – change from two shillings.

Half-pink draught cider – five pence.

A south-east London V-Day celebration photograph: long table in the open air, benches, plates of Viennese whirls on the table; paper chains with paper bells between houses; women in Juliet caps, little girls still in crocheted winter hats, a boy staring at the camera, displaying mannequin legs in long, dark stockings with lines of jonquil brightness in them.

A photograph of a brother in a Crombie, with gurning mouth and whimsical hair, like Kenneth Williams in *Carry On Sergeant.*

A trip with that brother from Victoria to Seattle, ship going under Golden Lion Bridge, the whimsical hair seduced in Eastman Colour to henna, the flat of Canada with its cherry maple leaf blowing.

'And it came to pass in an eveningtide, that David arose from off his bed, and walked upon the roof of the King's house: and from the roof he saw a woman washing herself; and the woman was very beautiful to look upon … and she came in with him and he lay with her …'

A Jugendstil lamp in Café Remember partly lights up Rembrandt's lover Hendrickje Stoffels modelling as Bethsheba: nude, distended belly, drop earrings, parure in hair, right foot meekly submitted for washing by an elderly woman in Reformation black.

The face of the girl from Galway City comes back, wheaten strands of hair, bow lips.

Recently in London I'd met a boyfriend of hers, also from Galway City, who'd had lots of breakdowns – his curly hair grey but his face still young and rosy like the pinks in a countrywoman's lapel.

He was wearing insect eyeglasses and a striped Grandad shirt.
Taking a course in the University of London he told me.

A barge goes by on Singel Canal with a band of about eighteen accordion players, women and boys, in white and black, all playing and some of them singing 'Sing Nactigall, Sing.'

'The answer is yes. Yes. Yes.

You were right to do it. You were right to live the life you have lived.

There are brain cells that are ill, that are irrevocably sick.

You can't have a real child. You wouldn't want to pass on this disease to another human being.

But you can in spite of everything, in spite of all, have a spiritual child.

You can choose some face, an expression, and follow that face.

In spite of them, you can still be a father to some son.'

The ultramarine and lemon train to Zandvoort aan Zee, passes Circus Kastello, young men with naked torsos, in tall mock-crocodile boots, outside it.

Through a window at Zandvoort aan Zee I look at a table ready for dining, a small Bible at each place.

On the beach a man drives an American harness racer against the sunset.

The Sisters of Mercy, founded in Dublin by Catherine Elizabeth McAuley, came to our town in the middle of the nineteenth century.

When I was a child they visited poor families at Christmas, brought packets of tea, sugar: boxes of Fox's Speciality – a family of chocolates and caramel-covered biscuits on ambler-purple featured on the box.

Mrs Mulloy visited Australia once.

Near Brisbane, Queensland, was a vast field of graves of Mercy nuns, and near it a vast field of graves of priests. Many of the nuns and priests had died in their early twenties of malaria and other diseases.

'I'm one of the forty-niners,' a Mercy man said to Mrs Mulloy in the field of Mercy nun graves.

'You came in 1949?'

'I came on a ship with forty-eight other nuns.'

In Etruria the patera in the hands of sarcophagi – saucer – represented continuity.

In London Hampsted Heath had been my patera.

When I first arrived in London in 1970, after getting a bedsit with a divan in Kilburn where a family of pub-wreckers called Looby from Southill in Limerick had reigned through the sixties, I went to Hampstead Heath, saw the plum tree at Keats' Grove under which Keats wrote 'Ode to the Nightingale'.

It was an overcast late afternoon in July and many of the houses on the margin of the Heath were lighted up.

Houses with lozenge shapes in the transoms; Japanese red maple trees, Chinese lantern trees with their red flowers, antler sumachs in cobbled yards.

I stared in the windows of other people's homes.

London remained other people's homes.

Since March – a blackthorn winter this year – I'd been swimming out to the coots' nest in a lifebuoy on the Men's Pond where the young were hatching – a large bowl of wet vegetation.

Patera – continuity.

A Polish man with a bull earring, in a T-shirt patterned with sunglasses, speaks to me.

He came to Amsterdam in the sixties from Rzeszow, South Poland where the apples taste like strawberries, and he works in a hospital. Worked with the first Aids cases in Amsterdam. Cycled to visit them.

Saw the excrement all over the bedsheets in the apartments with such objects as a Chinese boy with a pear of hair on top of his bald head, sitting on an amber fish, or an old Chinese woman kissing the nude breast of a young Chinese woman.

His family in Lech Walensa's Poland have completely rejected him and broken off contact with him because he's gay.

He lives with a young man he met in Nieuwe Meer Park on the southern outskirts of Amsterdam. But it's devastatingly lonely at Christmas when his friend goes to his family and he's alone in an apartment that has images of the nude male body by Wilhelm von Gloedon and André Kertész and walnut fold-up chairs called Savonarola or Dante chairs that the Florentines used either carry on their campaigns or use for reading and writing.

Like Kurt Cobain he has a tattoo from Hanky Panky – the Igala Native American totem golden eagle. Symbol of flight.

I am in another place, Iowa, with its Native American mound sites.

An Amish couple in a buggy against the September corn, the man in a broad brimmed black hat, jacket fastened with hooks and eyes, the woman in Pilgrim Father's bonnet, black dress and black shawl.

I met a woman with Grace Kelly blonde hair who ran away from her Amish home as a teenager and we went back together in her Hudson coupé to her gingerbread village where an English known as Pennsylvania Dutch is spoken and we walked together under the post oak trees and the tulip trees and the autumn maple trees.

'He is the Rock, his work is perfect …'

An old American man, just back from Eastern Europe, on a boat on the Mississippi, head in hands, the waspish hair that covers his head albino-white, a Chinese man, who in the 1980s had to burn all his manuscripts, diaries, notes in China, singing Chinese opera, the American flag blowing, yellow leaves on the boat.

A group photograph by a picture window against the cornfields. Bottle of white Grenache on the table. A Chinese woman, the old man's wife, in a melon stole with tassels, big loops of glasses, bent over laughing, a taciturn boy with gold of Ophir hair beside her.

The gargantuan apartment block in which I stayed looking towards a Native American mound.

South-east London where I moved after Iowa was always lonely for me.

There was six months in Berlin, a feast in May with a German boy with a lost koala bear face like Enzo Staiola – the child-actor who played the little boy in Vittorio De Sica's *Bicycle Thieves*, Armani-model cockscomb, who was to die of Aids a month later – the buildings of Kreuzberg amber in the sunset.

There's been another German boy present, in a shirt with green and yellow sunburst pattern, a student who looked a cross between Achim von Arnim, the neo-classical faced poet who wrote a poem about a youth who brought the empress a magic horn and Daniel Cohn-Bendit (Red Dani) : later he killed himself by slashing his wrists in the Gironde on a summer trip.

The old man on the boat on the Mississippi was to come to see me during a trip to Berlin but he died before leaving for Europe at O'Hare airport in Chicago.

'Then a boat trip up the Rhine to Bonn-Mainz, where my one remaining German relative will meet us and for five days we will drive around the Black Forest and visit the small town from which my ancestors emigrated to Iowa.'

European burial sites of the third and fourth centuries were found to contain glass medallions backed with gold leaf, engraved with bone. Pre-Prohibition America adopted this technique in its pub mirrors, enhancing it.

It was as if Iowa and Berlin were gilded into one another like parts of a mirror in a pre-Prohibition pub.

In the mirror I see the face of the boy who died of Aids. Just before he died he looked more composed than ever: pink ochre, circle-necked jersey, nylon-black hair.

'It's the inner freedom. Lose that and you're dead anyway.'

When I first came to live in south-east London an English boy from New York – a goliard (wandering scholar), with so many slashes on his jeans and so much flesh showing it looked as if a lion had been eating his jeans, came to visit me.

It was just after Christmas and the William IV box-shaped house was covered in rime – hoar frost.

He sang a song for me about Robin Hood.

Robin Hood meets a Tinker with a crab-tree staff and a warrant for his arrest. Robin Hood takes him to a Nottingham pub where he gets the Tinker drunk on ale and wine and then absconds, leaving

the Tinker with the ten-shilling bill. The Tinker finds Robin Hood
in the woods, hunting deer, and instead of attacking him, joins him.

My friend from Germany had stayed with me over Christmas.

I was invited to a party in West London that Christmas day. I
wore a cardigan for it that was the colour of the night sea off Palestine where I'd been the previous autumn, having taken up an invita-
tion given to me in Iowa.

I was afraid to bring my friend, thinking it would be rude. But
they were aware of him and there was a place set for him with his
name on the table.

A woman in gold, stretch-lamé evening dress had danced with a
soldier in Royal Welch Fusiliers uniform.

I'd been alone against the Mediterranean the previous autumn
– the walled city of Acca, a tight fistful of stars over the sea, areca
palms near the port, voices on the dark streets.

A hoard of gold and silver, excavated at the site of Troy, north-
western Turkey in 1873, said to have belonged to Priam, King of Troy
and brother of Ganymede who was singled out on Mount Ida by
Zeus for his beauty, missing from Berlin since World War II, turns
up in Moscow.

Ganymede ultimately became a star identified by Galileo and
named by Simon Marius.

The sunset at Zandvoort aan Zee is gone now. The journey is a
dead-end. There is no country.

My only country is the flag of postcards on the wall – whatever
they may happen to be.

But the continuity – the saucer, the patera – continues: Hampstead Heath, Zandvoort aan Zee, cornfields of Iowa, a walk into a
November sunset, with the American flag and a flag with the Wild
Rose of Iowa blowing over the pumpkins and a look back onto a
house, where we were served cranberry pudding based on a recipe in
Mrs Leslie's Cookbook, where someone who claimed he had a piece of
Dolly Parton's wig had just sung 'My Tennessee Mountain Home',
flaring like someone pulling a cigarette in the night – one of life's few
houses of friendship.

From the Town

In the grape-hyacinth-blue jersey – yellow stripe at V-neck, blue tie, navy trousers of Kinsale Community School, Wesley Loramar would wait in cubicles at the public lavatory at the beginning of Pier Road, Kinsale, aged sixteen, with the look of the bored cherub in Raphael's *The Madonna of San Sisto*.

Kinsale, with its whaling frame houses, was where the pirate Anne Bonny was from.

Anne's lawyer father, William Cormac, got a servant girl, Peg Brennan, pregnant. The three fled to Charleston, North Carolina, where William became a planation owner.

When she was thirteen Anne stabbed a servant girl. At sixteen she married and went off with James Bonny, a pirate. On the sea she had a homosexual companion, Pierre Bouspeut.

She decided to elope with another pirate, John ' Calico' Rackham. On the ship *Revenge* she met Mark Read who was really Mary Read and they became lovers.

The ship was captured October 1720, the men executed, the two women spared because they claimed pregnancy.

Wesley, wheaten and auburn hair, Titian-red eyebrows, body like a military road, hoping to be picked up, would be seen hitchhiking in a school uniform on the Inishannon Road, three miles north-west of Kinsale, close to Dunderrow, not far from the Bandon River.

Dunderrow — fortress of oak plain.

There is an American chemical factory there now.

Coins left by Elizabeth's forces before the Battle of Kinsale 1601 have been found here.

In yesteryears Mrs Harrington would travel by pony and trap from Kinsale each day to teach here, picking up pupils on the way.

Her pony was cared for while she was teaching by the Bowen family.

A man named Billy the Butler owned the local manor just prior to Mrs Harrington's career.

Bankruptcy had dogged successive owners of that manor and he too went bankrupt.

Wesley would be seen coming out of Dunderrow Wood, which had the sow-like smell of lesser celandine in spring — slight moustache like the down inside the foxglove — where he'd lain with workers from the chemical factory. He was like Orpheus who stole their husbands from the Thracian women.

Some said he'd been doing this since he'd worn the grey jumper and grey trousers of Saint John's National School.

Some even said he'd once been seen coming out of the wood in red PE jersey of Saint John's.

Sometimes too he'd be seen hitchhiking at Ballythomas Cross Road.

They described him at Kinsale Community School as *aireach* (gay), *le na pucaí* (with the fairies, gay).

They described him as a white-headed boy.

On his wall in Saint Joseph's Terrace was one of Elizabeth Peyton's portraits of John Lennon: toy-boy John Lennon in shirt with winged collars, aquamarine starry tie against a cranberry background with lightings. And Wesley did not look unlike an Elizabeth Peyton portrait himself.

He made love to a member of Trinity College Rowing Club, with frog green and tadpole brown mix eyes and a ginger lighting of pubic hair who gave him a Trinity Rowing Club jacket as a reward — the words Dublin University Rowing Club on it.

Wesley went to England, saw boys doing striptease in police uniform, soldier's uniform, sailor's uniform, Black Watch kilts and

Balmorals, boys naked but for motorboard hats.

'Before the street is full of terrors ...'

When there was nail-bomb attack on the Admiral Duncan Pub in Old Compton Street, Soho – lilac fascia, Admiral with silver cowslick and water-green lining to his coat – killing a pregnant girl and two men, people wrapped in thermal blankets under Saint Patrick's Church, Wesley left England.

On his return, in white, New Age kilt, plaid cap with prince's plume, black work boots, he'd walk on the headland by Foxes' Cave, as far as the Block House, with its iron-barred windows, from which they'd put pontoons and chains to the other side of the Estuary, during James II's stay, to prevent ships from entering the harbour.

As it was May the headland was blue and gold – Stuart colours – bluebells, buttercups.

The *Lusitania*, named after a district in Spain, was sunk off the old gold Old Head of Kinsale May 1915, 1198 lives lost, including that of Hugh Percy Lane – willowy, mushroom-eared, moustachioed – who bequeathed paintings by Renoir, Monet, Degas, Manet, Vuillard to Ireland.

Fond of needlework as a Cork Church of Ireland rector's young son, owned a rose-diamond hair ornament of Marie Antoinette's, an unsigned codicil in his will the subject of a bitter quarrel between England and Ireland.

The Unionist MP Harford Montgomery Hyde, whom Ian Paisley wanted condemned by the Orange Order for suggesting William of Orange was gay, argued for the return of the pictures from London to Dublin.

Two Irish students in beat jerseys removed one of them – a Berthe Morisot (she herself painted by both Manet and Renoir) – from the Tate Gallery.

Eventually the paintings were shared, including one that was on Wesley's wall in the neighbourhood of John Lennon – Renoir's *Les Parapluies*: girl with flaming marigold hair, in lavender dress, besieged by violet umbrellas.

Wesley would return to town by Compass Hill, past the convent-boarding school.

The nuns got old. No vocations. And they closed it.

When Michael Jackson was accused of molesting a thirteen-year-old boy in 2003 when they were sleeping together at Jackson's home in Santa Barbara County, of letting young adolescents get wild at his ranch, drinking alcohol, sleeping with him, Wesley's career, though he was now twenty-one, became more difficult, because he still looked so young.

Eyes the green brown of summer canal silt, moon adolescent nipples when he took off his shirt by Croadhoge Point.

Wesley would sometimes follow the heron on walking trips up river.

The Bandon River is full of stone crossing points. Three miles the other side of Bandon Town is a footbridge that capsized in a storm. Bittersweet – yellow and purple flowers – flourishes here.

A sparkling white little egret is said to come to this spot for winter.

Mostly deserted for a few years, it was here Wesley met Ciaran Crummey, aged sixteen, who'd decided it was a good swimming place.

Auburn hair, kingfisher orange undergrowth to chin. Freckles on his face like an orchard of very red apples – his head an auburn cannonball.

The tattoo Ciaran with diaeresis on C and N at the back of his neck.

'Your one gets small after you swim,' he told Wesley. 'My one stays big.' His 'tool-box' he called this area.

'I'm fighting with all the Poles in Bandon Town and they're fighting with me. I punched one in the face and he had to get seven stitches.'

They started meeting here regularly.

There'd been a reformatory school in Bandon run by Brothers and a man on Bandon Bridge with a lion tamer's moustache, always watching the Protestant heron in the river – draperies like a dowager, taking a very refined drink after devouring a snail or a fish – had been put in there as a boy and had told Ciaran about it.

'Poor boys and orphans were sent there. The other boys used mould carbolic soap in the shape of a penis and put it up twelve and thirteen year old boys' anuses and they'd have sex with the boy. Maybe four of them.

If a boy objected they'd gag his mouth with carbolic soap in a sock.'

Ciaran stood against the river after repeating this story, a dun penumbra to the crack of his buttocks.

One day two of the Bandon 'shams' — one like an owl in an Argos chain, the other with face like a conger eel — saw Wesley and Ciaran make love through the wych elm, whereupon Ciaran promptly claimed he'd been raped.

Wesley was now twenty-four although he looked almost younger than Ciaran.

Two guards like lapett-faced vultures — the ones with wattled and naked crimson heads — sat on either side of Wesley in court waiting to take him away.

Wesley got a six months' custodial sentence.

First he was taken to Limerick Jail where he had to share a cell with a drug dealer with the words Pray for Better Days, tattooed on his right arm in biro and ink.

There was an inventory of Wesley's possessions. A black jersey he'd bought at Christopher New's in Soho was confiscated because he'd look like a warden in it and could get out.

His palm prints were taken.

Then he was taken in a patrol wagon to Cork Jail where a man on a sexual offence, with tattoo of the Grim Reaper from *The Salted Sea* on his back, had a fabliau for Wesley:

'There used to be a lavatory behind the Opera House in Cork. I went there one night when *Thoroughly Modern Millie* was playing at the Opera House and then I went to the other lavatories. When I returned that night to the one behind the Opera House it was bull-dozed.'

From Cork Wesley was transferred to Arbour Hill Dublin associated with the draconian sentences of the Revolutionaries of 1916, where a young Croatian, who'd been involved in clean-up operations in Bosnian villages when he was fifteen, commended him on what he had done: 'Everyone must have the balls to do something against the law. In prison you'll see if you're a man or a pussy.'

Wesley spent a short while in adjacent Mountjoy.

A man had recently been murdered here.

In Mountjoy Wesley met Eadric Hepplewhite, half Romany, half

Pakistani. Chocolate bonbon eyes, teeth black as the spherical King Alfred's cakes tree fungus.

Stirbin Eadric called jail. He'd previously known two stirbins – Edmonds Hill Prison Suffolk and HMP Lewes, where he'd worn an orange top and blue trousers in both.

He was from Uckfield, East Sussex, where they'd lived in a Reading Romano vardo with pears, apples lions' heads embossed on the front and mugs on the dresser with the young Beatles faces on them.

His father used hunt the badger with coal in his shoes to prevent the badger biting his feet and breaking the bones.

They'd come to Ireland after Eadric's spells in prison.

Lived in Gort, County Galway, at Greg London's camping site opposite Texaco Garage on the Limerick Road.

So many young Brazilians working in the meat factory there, they'd formed an entire soccer team!

Then they'd lived in a highrise, Ballymun, north Dublin.

Grazed a Gypsy vanner there.

'Me and the boys would turn the steering wheel to the left or the right on an edge in the fields of Ballymun and it would flip over. I'd joyride anything. Trucks.

Anything.

When I was first put in the Joy a woman from Ballymun used visit me. Used bring me packages. Used bring me coconut oil. Said she loved me.'

Free again, Wesley walked up the Bandon River to the spot where he used meet Ciaran Crummey.

Like the red-crested green woodpecker that turns a faded brown in summer, like the pied woodpecker with red spot on head, who announces itself in spring with a rapid drum-roll, like the crow-sized black woodpecker who feeds on the pincer-horned Hercules ants, nude boys are not to be found in Ireland.

There were woodpeckers in this land once but they vacated it.

What kind of woodpecker Wesley wondered nursed Romulus and Remus by the Tiber under the Ficus Rominales – fig free of Romina, Goddess of nursing mothers?

The red-crested, lesser spotted woodpecker, smallest of the

woodpeckers, with strong barring, black and white, lives by rivers.

Wesley decided to leave Ireland.

'I'll away to fair England

Whatever may betide ...'

But first he'd go looking for Eadric Hepplewhite.

He stayed in a hotel in Dublin run by a dentist from Bournemouth.

A boy who looked like a Vieux Carré voluptary came back with him his first night.

Mandatory rose tattoo of Crumlin, south-west Dublin, at fourteen. Seduced by his best friend's father when he was fifteen, who was wearing construction gear.

He liked uniforms against him ever since. Especially Garda uniforms.

'They're only schoolboys. Trying to make a name for themselves.'

Had mother in Chinese tattooed on his right arm and a Japanese koi fish on his right thigh. But the rose tattoo was still there, faded near the Chinese lettering.

Wesley took the 13 bus to Ballymun.

'How's your dog?' a man with dropped ears like a Staffordshire bullterrier asked a man with facial scar like the Joker in Batman, on the bus.

'Collie?'

'No. The Alsatian.'

'He died.'

'How's that?'

'He was seventeen.'

'One dog is as good as another. I have an Alsatian-greyhound crossbreed. Hairy on front. A greyhound behind. Jumps over the wall. Terrifies everyone in Ballymun. He even frightens Fat Freddie Thompson.'

The Hepplewhites were no longer living in Ballymun, a woman who looked like Gina Lollobrigida adrift from her era, in a dress patterned with Calamity Janes in various poses – on horseback, prostrate, sitting on stiles, sharp shooting – and cactuses that appeared to have nipples, told Wesley.

'It's a complicated city,' Wesley commented looking at discarded electric coolers and discarded electric heaters.

'It's mental,' the woman replied.

Wesley searched Smithfield Sunday Horse Market for Eadric.

They were selling colour pictures of Reading Romany vardos, of Bedlington terriers, Scottish Lucas terriers, Irish Staffordshire terriers, Border terriers, Chihuahuas, Irish deer hounds, Aylesbury ducks.

An Indian man purchased a picture of Travellers in sixties clothes and the tartan an Antrim vicar met Traveller women in, in the 1670s.

Horse trappings were sold.

Strawberry-roan vanners, heavy black and white stallions, buck-skin American quarter horses, miniature Falabella Argentinian horses – descended from horses brought to Argentina by Andalusians, from herds of the Mapuche Indians in southern Buenos Aires province, from Crillo stock – harnessed to sulkies, mini-broughams, carts.

Welsh ponies tethered to beech trees.

A small Traveller boy who looked like an Easter chick galloped on a red, leopard-spotted Shetland-Appaloosan pony.

An Indian boy who drove from Belfast sold dinkie pork pies and bread-and-butter pudding with raisins soaked in Bushmills whiskey.

Smell of pizza, porchetta, panini.

Many of the boys had a spit of hair at the nape of their necks like the stamens of Saint John's Wort used in East Sussex for hairdressing.

A teenage, maple-syrup faced Romanian boy played 'The Wild Colonial Boy' on a Ballodi accordion while a Traveller boy with Cleopatra's asp hairstyle – shaven sides, cable on top – sang the words.

Jack Duggan, an only son from Castlemaine, County Kerry, where Traveller boys commit suicide in dozens now, usually by hanging themselves, left for a life of banditry in Australia at sixteen, was felled by the bullet of FitzRoy.

James McPherson – the Egyptian – had played his fiddle on the gallows at Banff, Scotland, in 1700.

A Traveller boy with a porky dog face in Brendan's Café on Mary's Lane, where there was a poster of the young Elton John dressed as an undertaker, but in black, high boots, told Wesley that Eadric had moved to Finglas.

There was heavy gang warfare at the moment between Finglas gangs and Raheny gangs.

Raheny gangs wore a red ribbon in their lapels. Finglas gangs wore a diamond stud in their ears.

At the entrance to the estate:

John Mouse Lee Karl R.I.P.

And:

Heartbreak.

'It's been terrible here the last few weeks,' a woman with bleached blonde hair, pancake face make-up, hare-lip, deliberately ripped jeans, wheeling a baby in fluff jacket like a marshmallow hedgehog, said to Wesley. 'Murders. They were blowing up houses. Blowing up Travellers' trailers.

I had this child by Smudgy. He was in jail. In the Midlands. They let him out. They said: "You're drug free now!"'

Wesley found Eadric in a flat with a Welsh cob in it.

Eadric had brought his horse into the house and tied him to the banister when local boys began climbing over the wall or leaning over the wall and sticking cider bottles up the horse's anus.

The crest of Eadric's hair was now dyed the orange of the florets of the red-hot poker flower and his black cargo trousers dipped to show a provocative display of floral print underwear.

Under a snow-leopard print light shade with boat feather borders, sitting on a cushion with shaven-headed Raw on it, were two fourteen-year-old boys snogging, one from Stirrup Lane near Smithfield Market, one from Coolock, north-east Dublin.

The one from Coolock had long, side-swept, japanned bangs, stud through lower mouth, wore mouse-grey, wine-rimmed Vans skate shoes, and was affecting the mannerisms of an Acapulco cross-dresser.

The one from Stirrup Lane wore a poppy-and-black lined Bohemians shirt.

Eadric agreed to accompany Wesley to England.

The Pennines irradiated with cottongrass.

First they went to the Appleby Horse Fair in the Westmorland fells.

A piebald, Appaloosan crossbreed was washed in the River Eden — markings like blue poppies.

Gypsy boys favoured borders hairstyle — messy top, shaven sides with outlines on front and behind the ears.

Young Romany boys like corbies gathered at Low Cross, a water pump near it around where two hiring fairs were held in the Middle Ages.

Irish Traveller boys ascended Gallows Hill as they would Mount Krizevac in Bosnia & Herzegovina, which has a cement cross on top, with blue and brown and pink rosaries around their necks.

'Times have changed. Romany girls like to show their minges.'

Romany girls with butter-brandy midriffs paraded the town in Queen Hippolyte coin-girdles. Denim hot pants with bibs — one strap unfastened. Reflector-yellow high heels. Silver spike heels.

Some had Pocahontas — squaw — hairstyle and dress.

A farrier shod a mottled, champagne horse with hot shoe that smoked in the sleet, while the Gypsy boy owner looked on in oilskins.

A sulky was drawn against the snow-capped June fells by a cream-coated Cremello horse, three youths in it, the ones on the outer sides with arms entwined about one another.

'There's snow on the Derbyshire peaks in July,' Eadric told Wesley. 'They speak Bram there.'

They drove south, crossing the Ribble River which once formed the southern border of the kingdom of Northumbria.

'Where hast thou been since I saw thee?

On Ilkley Moor without thy trousers?'

The oystercatchers live on the moors now, building their nests in railway ballast.

It would be a long time before Wesley would return to the town he was from, where Madame Rose and Madame Sylvia told fortunes in summer, and the Palomino horses of Piper's Funfair went around to mariache music, with Old Kinsale Head nearby where you often felt you could hear the foghorn of the *Lusitania* coming from far out at sea — like a question about Renoir who'd compared himself to a swallow following a gnat.

The History of Magpies

Every summer my mother would meet a Monsignor cousin of hers who had a face with embonpoint, in the Prince of Wales Hotel in Athlone.

The Monsignor worked in the Archbishop's Chancellery in Dublin.

She always brought me.

She'd wear her white dress stencilled with patterns of outlined swallows, or her purple dress with large terracotta flowers and smaller pale blue and white ones.

Her lips would be daubed in lipstick the crimson lake of the cover of the *Messenger of the Sacred Heart*, and she'd get drunk with the Monsignor on Ernest and Julio Gallo White Grenache.

They'd grown up together in a canalside village in County Westmeath and attended together the Eucharistic Congress in June 1932 where they'd been given rosaries by a French cardinal and had heard Count John McCormack sing 'Panis Angelicus' in the Phoenix Park.

The Monsignor worked strenuously with Archbishop John Charles McQuaid — who looked like a cross between one of the titanium, forked-faced prominenti burying the Count of Orgaz in an El Greco painting and the termagant who advertised Odearest Mattresses — to curb the Irish libido.

Two of his enterprises had been the Mambo Club in the Swiss

Chalet Ballroom in Santry, north Dublin, and the Yugoslav–Irish soccer match in Dalymount Park, Dublin, both in 1955.

The Mambo Club opened on Wednesday, 9 February 1955, to music by Jim Cook and his band, with vocals by the Jones Boys.

A Teddyboy club with drape-coats, stove-pipe trousers, Eton Clubman chukka boots with 3/8 soles, strings of pearls, wide-spreading sun-ray pleated skirts or moiré skirts, stilletto-heeled court shoes, toreador pants. Jitterbugging, shimmying.

One hundred Teddyboys each week and music by Earl Gill of the Palm Court Ballroom Orchestra.

With the help of my mother's cousin, John Charles McQuaid had it shut down by July of that year.

October – Ireland was to play Yugoslavia in Dalymount Park.

Cardinal Aloysius Stepinać, Archbishop of Zagreb, who'd advised Utaše leader Ante Pavelić during the Second World War, had been sentenced to sixteen years' forced labour in Lepoglava Prison – though the sentence was now commuted to house arrest – where he would be poisoned.

Schoolboys were forbidden to attend under pain of mortal sin.

In spite of this 21,400 supporters turned up to see the Yugoslav players cross themselves in unison as they emerged from the tunnel – some with Roman Catholic blessing, some with three-finger Greek Orthodox blessing, one with two-finger Raskolnik – Old Believer – blessing.

One late summer day my mother brought me to the Chancellery in Drumcondra.

Earlier that day I'd been sliding down the rainbow rocket into Dún Laoghaire Baths.

By the sea front there'd been a funfair with pictures on the billboards of Hutterite boy, a Scheherazade with triple-row necklace, a Jewish patriarch, a Jewish boy in kippa, Jayne Mansfield giving gung-ho salute.

My mother had bought me to see *The Loves of Hercules* in the red plush of the Regent Cinema on Parnell Street, where Colleen Mixture sweets and chocolate satins and chocolate Brazil nuts were sold, which had starred Jayne Mansfield in the twin roles of Hippolyte, Amazon queen, and Queen Deianeira.

There were sufficient myths embroiled in that film to lead one through a lifetime, as Dante was proverbially led by Virgil in Hades.

Hercules diverting the rivers Alphaeus and Peneius so they flowed through the cattle stables of King Augeas of Elis. His seizing of the cattle of the Giant Geryon with six heads, six hands, three torsos. The capture of the Cretan bull with flaming breath.

Hermes, the maker of Orpheus' lyre, stealing Apollo's cattle and making them walk backwards so their tracks would not betray where they'd gone.

The stealing of the girdle of Hippolyte.

Omphale, Queen of Lydia, dressing the enslaved Hercules as a woman, setting him to spinning, spanking him. Successfully fighting the river god Achelous for Queen Deianira, but she becoming jealous of another love, Iole, daughter of King Eurytus, and sending Hercules a shirt smeared in the blood of Nessus the centaur, who Hercules had slain, which she believed to be a love charm but which turned out to be a deadly poison, driving Hercules around Greece in pain, causing him to immolate himself, his immortal part rising to Mount Olympus, his mortal part ascending in smoke to the Heavens where he becomes the constellation Hercules.

In the Chancellery a nun with a face the yellow of an old wether brought us tea in cups with gold fruit, purple flowers on them, tea cake and currant slices in a room with burgundy carpet with fleur-de-lis pattern.

On the mantlepiece was a picture of St Margaret Mary of the Visitation Order, hands crossed under the cruxifix on her breast as if she was shielding that part of her body, beside a colour-tinted photograph of the Old Weir Bridge, Killarney. Above these a mandorla – oval – of the Assumption.

My mother was wearing a pale-blue dress with scarlet, deep azure, dun, olive-yellow bird on boughs in white blossom.

The Monsignor, possibly wishing to discuss a private matter, informed me there was a tree with Bergamot pears in the apple orchard – the seeds brought from France – and that I should go and pick some.

A small garden with pale-pink Penstemon, Gallega with blue-tinged, violet flowers, purple Allium, Ponytail Grass: then the orchard.

I identified the pear tree and climbed it and was commencing to pick the luscious, fat pears when John Charles McQuaid approached in cigarette trousers, black polo neck, clerical drape coat, and issued a rook-like hoarse yell, believing he'd caught a thief.

I was like Zacchaeus up the sycamore tree when he encountered Jesus.

I protested my connections, whereupon John Charles McQuaid, his left shoulder held higher than right – a touch of Quasimodo, a little like Seneca with his terribilità, whom he'd studied when he was a young priest who looked like St Gabriel Possenti, the damerino, the ladies' priest – asked me:

'What is your favourite miracle?'

'Fatima,' I replied.

'I'm disappointed it's not the Incarnation,' he said, 'How does Lourdes rate in your opinion?'

I said nothing.

'Do you know that Bernadette was canonized not because of the apparitions but because of her piety and faith?'

Again I was silent.

'Do you know that France is called the Eldest Daughter of the Church? St Veronica brought relics of the Blessed Virgin there and is buried in France.'

When he referred to the Eldest Daughter of the Church I had an image of the gleeman Jimmy O'Dea in a pongee singing 'Biddy Mulligan the Pride of the Coombe' and 'Daffy the Belle of the Coombe' in the pantomine at the Gaiety Theatre the previous Christmas.

My mother and I stayed in the Castle Hotel on Denmark Street with its gold lettering in the transom.

I'd slept in my mother's arms in pyjamas with a bouquet print.

The Archbishop took sudden note of a magpie, black with sailor blue, brilliant green, immaculate white.

'My favourite hobby is shooting magpies. I do it in my home, Notre Dame Des Bois in Killiney.'

Just as he would give a lesson to the boys at Blackrock College once, where he was known as Mixer McQuaid after Mick McQuaid Pipe Tobacco, he gave me a précis of the history of magpies in Ireland.

They'd arrived in Wexford in an easternly gale in 1676, two years before the Titus Oates Plot that led to the martyrdom of the Primate of All Ireland, Blessed Oliver Plunkett.

Magpies were first sighted in Dublin in 1852, the year John Henry Newman first arrived in Ireland.

George the Second had hated magpies and offered a penny for each one destroyed.

With the help of his favourite son, the Duke of Cumberland, he'd suppressed the Scottish rising.

But he'd supported Frederic Handel whose *Messiah*, beloved by McQuaid, was first performed in the New Musick Hall, Fishamble Street, Dubin, a few yards from Jimmy O'Dea's in the Coombe.

As his father before him had banned him from court, he banned his eldest son, Frederick Louis.

Perhaps he'd been touched in the head by the fact he'd once tried to visit his mother, Sophia Dorothea, who was imprisoned in a castle in the plains of Ahlden in northern Germany by George the First and wasn't allowed to see her.

McQuaid laughed gallicly at his joke.

'There was another of the Georges in the days of Sir Walter Scott known as Prinny, who slept all day, saw his ministers in his night-gown, and cried on their shoulders.'

Again he gave his gallic laugh.

His attention was diverted by another magpie.

'I wish I had my .22 rifle!'

There was a Parthian shot remark:

'Remember the path to Heaven is paved with mistakes.'

I had a vision of mistakes like the roses St Thérèse of Lisieux promised to shower the earth with after her death.

My mother's cousin and the Archbishop took a shot at another magpie some years later – Jayne Mansfield.

She was due to give a performance at the Brandon Hotel, Tralee, County Kerry.

On her way she'd stopped to light a candle in St Stephen's Church in Castleisland.

The entire population of Seanakill and Mitchel's Crescent, Tralee, had gathered on the Castleisland road to greet her.

Management of the Brandon Hotel bowed to McQuaid and my mother's cousin some hours before the performance and cancelled it.

Three months later Jayne Mansfield, Oscar-winning star of *The Wayward Bus*, in which she'd played stripper Camille Oaks who took her name from Camel cigarettes, was killed – a night drive from Mississippi to New Orleans.

On the small black and white television screen in our home, news broadcaster Charles Mitchell, with widow's peak, announced Jayne Mansfield's death in his sad voice as another oracle.

When Phryne the courtesan had been accused of blasphemy she'd bared her breasts to each of the jurors in the Areopagus – a hill in Athens – and they were so moved by them, her life was spared.

Giacomo Ceruti had painted a blonde Mary Magdalene, with skull.

The following year I visited France – Eldest Daughter of the Church.

I visited Notre Dame from which Quasimodo flung the wicked Claude Frollo, and I saw the body of St Bernadette at Nevers, who'd witnessed the Virgin on eighteen occasions by the Gave River.

My mother welcomed me back from France in a sky-blue dress patterned with green, yellow, dark blue, black, grey scooters.

When I read Stendhal's *The Charterhouse of Parma*, in the Penguin Classics edition with Ingre's portrait of Regency-style François Marius Granet on the jacket, in which the Virgin is party to love-making between an Archbishop and a girl, the girl having vowed to the Virgin only to make love to the Archbishop in the dark, so his face is never beheld and when she does accidentally see his face, peripeteia befalling all, I thought of John Charles McQuaid.

When I heard of his death I purchased a hardcover edition of *The Charterhouse of Parma*, with Hussar in a shako in the fray of the Battle of Waterloo on the jacket.

'The kingdom of God is a room,' said Catherine of Siena, who never learnt to write, and if it was a room there were many such rooms in London.

Bad news travels like flying feathers. On one of my visits back from a room in London they were gossiping about John Charles McQuaid.

A man claimed that when as a boy he was bringing McQuaid Jameson's Red Breast Malt Whiskey – crushed barley, ten years old – to an upstairs snug of a bar, McQuaid – wearing a beret and polo-neck jersey made a lurch at him. The Archbishop was a steamer!

McQuaid used to regularly return to Blackrock College, where the muse of rugby reigns, and the boys used to line up to kiss the Episcopal ring.

Shy with most people, he'd usually look away when they were kissing his ring, at the Blackrock boys he'd look directly.

Boys with bushy tops and short back and sides: Teutonic brows; Windsor ties – bow knot, diagonal across grain of the fabric and blades up to five inches; cable stitch, sleeveless jerseys; slim Ivy League style jackets from Switzer's; bubble bottoms in Scout Master length, vicuna trousers, tender cordovan shoes.

To the boys with slicked back, duck's arse hair style, with cowboy Slim Jim ties or small knot, square end ties, in crêpe-nylon poppy, acid yellow, acid green ankle socks, beetle squasher shoes, at Our Lady's Hostel, Eccles Street, McQuaid would come in his cramoisy gear.

The boys loved this gear.

Pomegranate red as in Sargent's portrait of Cardinal Newman with Angevin face.

A little of Jean Léon Gérôme's Cardinal Richelieu in his explosion of vermilion.

A lonely, lonely clerical or even papal Velázquez sitter who found companionship for an hour or so.

Like the girl in Stendhal's *The Charterhouse of Parma*, the homeless boys did not reject the Archbishop.

Perhaps John Charles McQuaid was like the Emperor in Hans Christian Andersen's story, who commissioned new clothes from two tailors, giving them silk and gold thread, they promising to make him wonderful new attire that would be invisible to the stupid, tricking him into parading nude, a child raising the cry that the Emperor was wearing no clothes.

Perhaps the boys at Our Lady's Hostel, Eccles Street, saw that John Charles McQuaid wore no clothes, that he was nude such as the nudes John Singer Sargent sketched or Thomas Eakins painted, who after losing his job because of his advocacy of male nudes, painted the portrait of the eighty-four-year-old Archbishop of Cincinnati, William Henry Elder — puce-purple biretta with black pompom, blackberry soutane — as the blackberries at the Pennsylvania swimming holes where he photographed the kindling nudity of his young male students — madder rose buttons, carnelian ring, autumn leaf coloured background, sad, remembering face.

'Nelly Kelly broke her belly
Sliding on a lump of jelly.'
A woman complained to my mother about me breaking in a skipping gait as I made my way on Society Street. A boy of my age skipping! What other things would I do in my life, if I did this now?

I return to Ireland after my years of absence.

What would previously have been a romantic furlough in a priest's or an Archbishop's life is now the subject of outcry.

Church paranoia of the past — studying ladies' underwear advertisements with magnifying glass to see if the mons veneris could be detected, objecting to nude models in Clery's window: religo-political paranoia — storming the Gate Theatre and threatening to burn it when Stalin's star, Orson Welles (who'd cast Eartha Kitt as Helen of Troy), was playing in Lion Feuchtwanger's *Jew Süss*, was turned into another and even more crazed direction.

No shopping centre and no park could be complete without a paedophile. If there wasn't a paedophile available, there had to be a Peeping Tom.

The Statute of Limitations did not apply to sex.

Murder, crucifixion — which literally happened in one case — were nothing compared to underage sex.

I meet old friends whom I don't feel want to talk to me. But I don't need their history. I have my own history. The history of aloneness.

The history of magpies. The history of aloneness. The history of my ancestry.

Penitential pilgrimages remembered back to the beginning of the nineteenth-century — dry bread, black tea, backs turned to the Cross of St Brigid, Patroness of the lactation of ewes, whose fire, in the Place of the Oak Tree in County Kildare, surrounded by a hedge of willow shoots, which no man could cross, was kept burning until the Reformation.

A person can die of loneliness, a person can die of a broken heart.

When I was a teenager I came across my father, who'd made this comment on John Charles McQuaid – 'He's not Mae West' – weeping. Sitting on his bed, face in hands.

He'd given me a set of art books and loose reproductions had gone with them. He was weeping in a corridor of masterpieces.

Jean Léon Gérôme. Marten van Heemskerck. Giacomo Ceruti.

Now I too was weeping in a corridor of masterpieces.

I cycle down Dorset Street where Cardinal Newman first stayed when he arrived in Dublin.

Past Trinity College from which McQuaid – otto' cento Irish cleric – banned Catholics, again under pain of mortal sin, which gave Samuel Johnson his doctor degree.

Past St Stephen's Green on which Gerald Manly Hopkins' room looked down. He used to wear a primrose on Primrose Day – 19 April – Disraeli's Memorial Day: they told him he may as well be wearing a cabbage.

Past Harcourt Street where Newman had a beautiful room in a double house with pagan alto-relievos on the wall; where Buck – Jerusalem – Whaley lived, who'd incurred a gambling debt of £14,000 in one evening in France when he was sixteen; where Gustavus Corn-wall, secretary of the Irish Post Office (the Duchess), described by a Kerry newspaper as one of the lowest scum of the earth, had musical evenings with Mary Annes, including Malcolm Johnston, of a bakery family (the Maid of Athens), whom legend said had sex in the Gaiety Theatre with Captain Martin Kirwan of the Royal Irish Fusiliers (Lizzie).

'Teach me how to kiss, dear Fifi.'

Past St Philip & St James' Church of Ireland in Blackrock with its fir trees, pine trees, arbutus tree.

My first homosexual experience – naked torso of a Protestant boy during rehearsals for a performance of *Dracula* in a shed in a back lane in our town.

Not Bram Stoker's Dracula. Not one of Sheridan Le Fanu's Draculas. A swarm of like-minded girls fled at the sight of me as Dracula in a Protestant shed.

Past Blackrock College where the boys are immersing themselves in the mud during a game of rugby, like Brent geese.

The Protestant boy later went to a Protestant school in Dublin where the swimming instructor would say to boys who attempted to wear togs in the showers: 'You came into the world naked and you'll go into the showers naked.'

In Dún Laoghaire – Kingstown – a fifteen-year-old boy, with dyed, spiked Emo hair but eyes the blue of violets in a seminary garden, looks into my eyes. John Charles McQuaid used to advise seminarists to wash their genitals with Cussen's Soap.

A semi-detached house with cut granite features in Dalkey which John Henry Newman had moved into, September 1854, with Father Ambrose St John, after a stay at Kingston where troop ships could be seen crossing the bay on their way to Crimea.

He who believed the snapdragon on the walls of Trinity College, Oxford, an emblem of his eternal residence there.

In January, mahonia – yellow bell flowers – grows at the porticoed door. A spike of cotoneaster peeps through a rail. The valerian is still in bloom.

There is China tea plant in the hedge opposite and still some fuchsia flowers alongside the snowberries.

A grey squirrel holds a nut as if it was a ball in a rugby scrum.

Lord Forbes of Castletownford in County Longford had brought the grey squirrels to Ireland at the beginning of the twentieth century, and they defeated the red squirrels, but were unable to cross the Shannon to the west.

There are amber lightings in the transom.

A porpoise surfaces in the 'Dress of Gerontius' Killiney Bay below, after a feast of cod and whiting.

Apollo had turned himself into a dolphin at Delphi, thus its name.

Hadn't Victoria been represented on coins, bearing a trident?

More beautiful than Italy, more beautiful than Sicily, Newman said.

In September golden samphire, sea lavender, silver weed, restharrow.

And the burnt sienna of montbretia against the Mazarin blue of Carrigoona, Dwouce, Mount Malin, the Sugerloaf and the Little Sugarloaf.

He censured the Oratorian lay brother from here who proposed, while still in his habit, to a young lady in Birmingham Oratory and Newman had brought to Dalkey where he used to sing in the kitchen as he made haemorrhaging blackberry tarts.

'On Egypt's plains where flow the ancient Nile ...

... and swims the crocodile ...'

Sometimes someone would come to the door selling ballad sheets, such as those with the songs of the blind Zozimus of Faddle Alley in the Coombe, who sang of 'beauteous Dublin town' and of St Mary of Egypt, another Camille Oaks, who received the last rites after her fifty years in the desert, from Bishop Zozimus.

In Catholic Holland it is believed that a marriage performed on a grave will bring peace to the dead. Marten van Heemskerck, who painted Dionysian male nudes, left a bequest for couples who were willing to perform this ceremony on the slab of his tomb in Haarlem Cathedral.

They'd tried to dig up Newman's bones at Rednal, Edgbaston, to put them in Birmingham Cathedral, but they found his dust had commingled with that of Father Ambrose St John.

Kennedy

A nineteen-year-old youth is made to dig a shallow grave in waste ground beside railway tracks near Limerick bus station and is then shot with an automatic pistol.

Eyes blue-green, brown-speckled, of blackbird's eggs.

He wears a hoodie jacket patterned with attack helicopters.

Murdered because he was going to snitch – go to the guards about a murder he'd witnessed – his friend Cuzzy had fired the shot. The victim had features like a Western stone wall. The murder vehicle – a stolen cobalt Ford Kuga – set on fire at Ballyneety near Lough Gur.

The hesitant moment by Lough Gur when blackthorn blossom and hawthorns blossom are unrecognizable from one another, the one expiring, the other coming into blossom.

Creeping willow grows in the waste ground near Limerick bus station – as it was April male catkins yellow, with pollen, on separate tree small greenish female stamens. In April also whitlow grass that Kennedy's grandmother Evie used to cure inflammation near finger-nails and toenails.

In summer creeping cinquefoil grows in the waste ground.

He was called Kennedy by Michaela, his mother, after John F. Kennedy, and Edward Kennedy, both of whom visited this city, the latter with a silver-dollar haircut and tie with small knot and square ends. He must have brought a large jar of Brylcream with him, Kennedy's father, Bongo, remarked about him.

'When I was young and comely,
Sure, good fortune on me shone,
My parents loved me tenderly.'

A pious woman found Saint Sebastian's body in a sewer and had a dream he told her to bury him in the Catacombs.

Catacumbas. Late Latin word. Latin of Julian the Apostate who studied the Gospels and then returned to the Greek gods.

The Catacombs. A place to take refuge in. A place to scratch prayers on the wall in. A place to paint in.

Cut into porous tufa rock, they featured wall paintings such as one of three officials whom Nebuchadnezzar flung in the furnace for not bowing before a golden image of him in the plain of Dura in Babylon, but who were spared.

Three officials, arms outstretched, in pistachio-green jester's apparel amid flames of maple red.

The body of Sebastian the Archer refused death by arrows and he had to be beaten to death. Some have surmised the arrows were symbolic and he was raped.

As the crime boss brought Kennedy to be murdered he told a story:

'I shook hands with Bulldog who is as big as a Holstein Friesian and who has fat cheeks.

It was Christmas and we got a crate and had a joint.

He said "I have the stiffness."

He slept in the same bed as me in the place I have in Ballysimon.

In the morning he says "Me chain is gone and it was a good chain. I got it in Port Mandel near Manchester."

He pulled up all the bedclothes.

He says "I'll come back later and if I don't get me chain your Lexus with the wind-down roof will be gone."

He came back later but he saw the squad car – "the scum bags" he said – and he went away.

A week later I saw Cocka, a hardy young fellow, with Bulldog's chain, in Sullivan's lane.'

The crime boss, who is descended from the Black and Tans, himself wears a white-gold chain from Crete, an American gold ring larger as a Spanish grandee's ring, a silver bomber jacket and pointy shoes of true white.

He has a stack of *Nude* magazines in his house in Ballysimon, offers you custard and creams from a plate with John Paul II's – Karol Wojtyla's – head on it, plays Country and Western a lot.

Sean Wilson – Blue Hills of Breffni, Westmeath Bachelor.

Sean Moore – Dun Laoghaire can be such a Lonely Place.

Johnny Cash – I walk the Line.

Ballysimon is famed for a legitimate dumping site but some people are given money to dump rubbish in alternative ways. 'Millionaires from dumping rubbish,' it is said of them.

By turning to violence, to murder, they create a history, they create a style for themselves. The become ikons as ancient as Calvary.

Matthew tells us his Roman solder torturers put a scarlet robe on Christ, Mark and John – a robe of purple.

Emerging from a garda car Kennedy's companion and accomplice Cuzzy, in a grey pinstripe jersey, is surprised into history.

Centurion's facial features. A flick of hair to the right above his turf cut makes him a little like a crested grebe.

South Hill boys like Cuzzy are like the man-eating mares of King Diomedes of the Bistones that Hercules was entrusted to capture – one of the twelve labours King Eurystheus imposed on him.

'If I had to choose between Auschwitz and here,' he says of his cell, 'I'd choose Auschwitz.'

As Kennedy's body is brought to Janesboro church some of his brothers clasp their hands in attitude of prayer. Others simply drop their heads in grief.

Youths in suits with chest hammer pleats and cigarette-rolled shoulders. Mock snake-skin shoes. With revolver cufflinks.

One of the brothers has a prison tattoo – three Chinese letters in biro and ink – on the side of his right ear.

The youngest brother is the only one to demur jacket and tie, has his white shirt hanging over his trousers and wears a silver chain with boxing gloves.

Michaela's – Kennedy's mother – hair is pêle-mêle blanche-blonde, she wears horn-toed, fleur-de-lys-patterned, lace-up black high heels, mandorala – oval – ring, ruby and gold diamante on finger nails against her black.

Her businessman boyfriend wears a Savile-Row style suit chosen from his wardrobe of dark lilac suits, grey and black lounge suits, suits with black collars wine suits, plum jackets, claret-red velvet one-button jackets.

Kennedy's father Bongo had been a man with kettle-black eyebrows, who was familiar with the juniper berries and the rowan berries and the scarlet berries of the bittersweet – the woody nightshade – sequestered his foal with magpie face and Talmud scholar's beard where these berries, some healing, some poisonous, were abundant. He knew how to challenge the witch's broom.

John Joe Criggs, the umbrella mender in Kileely, used send boys who looked like potoroos – rat kangaroos with prehensile tails – to Weston where they lived, looking for spare copper.

'You're as well hung as a stallion like your father,' Bongo would say to Kennedy. 'Get a partner.'

In Clare for the summer he once turned to Michaela in the night in Kilrush during a fight.

'Go into the Kincora Hotel and get a knife so I can kill this fellow.'

He always took Kennedy to Ballyheigue at Marymass – 8 September – where people in bare feet took water in bottles from the Holy Well, left scapulars, names and photographs of people who were dead, children who'd been killed.

He fell in a pub fight. Never woke up.

His mother Evie had hung herself when they settled her.

Hair ivory grey at edges, then sienna, in a ponytail tied by velvet ribbon, usually in tattersall coat, maxie skirt, heelless sandals.

On the road she'd loved to watch the mistle thrush who came to Ireland with the Act of Union of 1801, the Wee Willie Wagtail – blue tit – with black eyestripes and lemon breast, the chaffinch with pink lightings on its breast who would come up close to you, in winter the frochán – ring ouzel, white crescent around its breast, bird of river, of crags.

On the footbridge at Doonass near Clondara she told Kennedy of the two Jehovah's Witnesses who were assaulted in Clondara, their Bibles burned, the crowd cheered on by the parish priest, and then the Jehovah's Witnesses bound to the peace in court for blasphemy.

Michaela's father Billser had been in Glin Industrial School. The Christian Brothers, with Abbey School of Acting voices, used get them to strip naked and lash them with the cat of the nine tails. Boys with smidgen penises. A dust, a protest of pubic hair. Boys with pubes as red as the fox who came to steal the sickly chickens, orange as the beak of an Aylesbury duck, brown of the tawny owl.

Then bring them to the Shannon when the tide was in and force them to immerse in salt water.

The Shannon food – haws, dulse, barnacles – they ate them. They robbed mangels, turnips. They even robbed the pig's and bonham's – piglet's – food.

'You have eyes like the blackbird's eggs. You have eyes like the *céirseach's* eggs. You have eyes like the merie's eggs, a Brother, nicknamed the Seabhac – hawk – used tell Billser.

Blue-green, brown-speckled.

He was called the Seabhac because he used to ravage boys the way the hawk makes a sandwich of autumn brood pigeons or meadow pipits, leaving a flush of feathers.

He had ginger-beer hirsute like the ruffous-barred sparrowhawk that quickly gives up when it misses a target, lays eggs in abandoned crow's nests.

A second reason for his nickname was because he was an expert in Irish and the paper-covered Irish dictionary was penned by *an Seabhac* – the Hawk.

Father Edward J. Flanagan from Ballymoe, north Galway, who

founded Boys Town in Omaha and was played by Spencer Tracy, came to Ireland in 1946 and visited Glin Industrial School.

The Seabhac gave him a patent hen's egg, tea in a cup with black-birds on it, Dundee cake on a plate with the same pattern.

Billser used cry salty tears when he remembered Glin.

Michael's grandfather Torrie had been in the British army and the old British names for places in Limerick City kept breaking into his conversation – Lax Weir, Patrick Punch Corner, Saint George's Street.

Cuzzy and Kennedy met at a Palaestra – boxing club.

Cuzzy was half-Brazilian.

'My father was Brazilian. He knocked my mother and went away.'

'Are you riding any woman now?' he asked Kennedy, who had rabbit-coloured pubes, in the showers.

'You have nipples like monkey fingers,' Kennedy said to Cuzzy, who has Palomino-coloured pubes, in the showers.

The coach, who looked like a pickled onion with tattoos in the nude, was impugned for messing with the teenage boxers. HIV Lips was his nickname.

'Used box for CIE Boxing Club,' he said of himself. 'Would go around the country. They used wear pink-lined vests, and I says no way am I going wear that.'

'He sniffed my jocks. And there were no stains on them,' a shaven-headed boxer who looked like a defurred monkey or a peeled banana, reported in denunciation of him.

A man who had a grudge against him used scourge a statue of the Greek boxer Theagenes of Thasos until it fell on him, killing him.

The statue was thrown in the sea and fished up by fishermen.

In the Palaestra was a poster of John Cena with leather wrap-pings on his forearm like the Terme Boxer – *Pugile delle Terme* – a first-century BC copy of a second-century BC statue that depicted Theagenes of Thasos.

John Cena in a black baseball cap, briefs showing above trousers beside a lingering poster for Circus Vegas at Two Mile Inn – a kick-boxer in mini-bikini briefs and mock-crocodile boots.

Kennedy and Cuzzy were brought to the garda station one night when they were walking home from the boxing club.

'They'll take anyone in tracksuits.'

Cuzzy, aged sixteen, was thrown in the girls' cell.

Kennedy was thumped with a mag lamp, a telephone book used to prevent his body from being bruised.

Cuzzy was thumped with a baton through a towel with soap in it.

A black guard put his tongue in Kennedy's ear. A Polish guard felt his genitals.

Kennedy punched the Polish guard and was jailed.

Solicitors brought parcels of heroin and cocaine into jail.

Youths on parole would swallow one eight heroin and fifty euro bags of heroin, thus sneak them in.

One youth put three hundred diazepam, three hundred steroid, three ounces of citric in bottle, three needles up his anus.

Túr Cant for anus.

Ríspún Cant for jail.

Slop out in mornings.

Not even granule coffee for breakfast. Something worse.

Locked up most of the day.

One youth with a golfball face, skin-coloured lips of the young Dickie Rock, when his baseball cap was removed, a pronounced bald patch on his blond head, had a parakeet in his cell.

Cuzzy would bring an adolescent Alsatian to the Unemployment Office.

Then he and Kennedy got a job laying slabs near the cement factory at Raheen.

Apart from work, Limerick routine.

Drugs in cling-foil or condoms put up their anuses, guards stopping them – fingers up their anuses.

Tired of the routine they both went to Donegal to train with AC armalite rifles and machine guns in fields turned salmon-colour by ragged robin.

The instructor had a Vietnam veteran pepper-and-salt beard and wore Stars and Stripes plimsolls.

The farmer who used own the house they stayed in would have a boy come for one month in the summer from an Industrial School, by arrangement with the Brothers.

The boy used sleep in the same bed as him and the farmer made him wear girl's knickers.

In Kennedy's room was a poster of Metallica – fuchsine bikini top, mini-bikini, skull locket on forehead, fuchsine mouth, belly button that looked like a deep cleavage of buttocks, skeleton's arms about her.

'It was on Bermuda's island
That I met with Captain Moore…'

'It's like the Albanians. They give you a bit of rope with a knot at the top.

Bessa they call it.

They will kill you or one of your family.

You know the Albanians by the ears. Their ears are taped back at birth.

And they have dark eyebrows.

I was raised on the Island.

You could leave your doors open. They were the nicest people.

Drugs spoiled people.'

Weston where Kennedy grew up was like Bedford-Stuyvesant or Brownsville New York where Mike Tyson grew up, his mother, who died when he was sixteen, regularly observing him coming home with clothes he didn't pay for.

Kennedy once took a 150 euro tag off a golf club in a Limerick store, replaced it with a 20 euro tag, and paid for it.

As a small boy he had a Staffordshire terrier called Daisy.

Eyes a blue coast watch, face a sea of freckles, he let the man from Janesboro who sucked little boys' knobs buy him 99s – the ice-cream cones with chocolate flake stuck in them, syrup on top, or traffic light cakes – cakes with scarlet and green jellies on the icing.

He'd play knocker gawlai – knock at doors in Weston and run away.

He'd throw eggs at taxis.

Once a taxi driver chased him with a baseball bat.

'I smoked twenty cigarettes since I was eleven.

Used work as a mechanic part-time then.

I cut it down to ten and then to five recently. My doctor told me my lungs were black and I'd be on an oxygen mask by the time I was twenty.

I'm nineteen.'

The youth in the petrol-blue jacket spoke against the Island on which someone on a bicycle was driving horses.

A lighted motorbike was going up and down Island Field.

We were on the Metal Bridge side of the Shannon.

It was late afternoon, mid-December.

'They put barbed wire under the Metal Bridge to catch the bodies that float down. A boy jumped off the bridge, got caught in the barbed wire and was drowned.

They brought seventeen stolen cars here one day and burned all of them.'

There were three cars in the water now, one upside down, with the wheels above the tide.

'When I was a child my mother used always be saying "I promised Our Lady of Lourdes. I promised Our Lady of Lourdes."

There's a pub in Heuwagen in Basel and I promised a friend I'd meet him there.

You can get accommodation in Paddington on the way for twenty pounds a night. Share with someone else.'

He turned to me. 'Are you a Traveller. Do you light fires?'

He asked me where I was from and when I told him he said, 'I stood there with seventeen Connemara ponies once and sold none of them.'

On his fingers rings with horses' heads, saddles, hash plant.

His bumster trousers showed John Galliano briefs.

Two stygian hounds approached the ride followed by an owner with warfare orange hair, in a rainbow hoodie jacket, who called 'Mack' after one of them.

He pulled up his jacket and underlying layers to show a tattoo Makaveli on his butter-mahogany abdomen.

'I got interested in Machiavelli because 2Pac was interested in him. Learnt all about him. An Italian philosopher. Nikolo is his first name. Put his tattoo all over my body. Spelt it Makaveli. Called my Rottweiler-Staffordshire terrier cross-breed after him. Mack.

Modge is the long-haired black terrier.

Do you know that 2Pac was renamed Tupac Amaru Shakur by his mother after an Inca sentenced to death by the Spaniards?

In Inca language: Shining Serpent.

Do you know that when the Florentines were trying to recapture Pisa Machiavelli was begged because he was a philosopher to stay at headquarters but he answered,' and the youth thrust out his chest like Arnold Schwarzenegger for this bit, 'that he must be with his soldiers because he'd die of sadness behind the lines?

They say 2Pac was shot dead in Los Vegas. There was no funeral. He's alive as you or me.

I'm reading a book about the Kray Twins now.

Beware of sneak attacks.'

And then he went off with Mack and Modge singing the song 2Pac wrote about his mother, 'Dear Mama.'

'When I was a child my father used take me to Ballyheigue every year.

There's a well there.

The priest was saying Mass beside it during the Penal Days and the Red Coats turned up with hounds.

Three wethers jumped from the well, ran towards the sea.

The hounds chased them, devoured them and were drowned.

The priest's life was spared.

They were of Thomond, neither or Munster of Connaught, Thomond bodies, Thomond pectorals.

The other occasion I met Kennedy was on a warm February Saturday.

He was sitting in a Ford Focus on Hyde Road in red silky football shorts with youths in similar attire.

He introduced me to one of them, Razz, who had an arm tattoo of a centurion in a G-string.

'I was in Cloverhill. Remand prison near a courthouse in Dublin. Then Mountjoy. You'd want to see the bleeding place. It was filthy. The warden stuck his head in the cell one day and "You're for Portlaoise." They treat you well in Portlaoise.'

'What were you in jail for?'

'A copper wouldn't ask me that.'

A flank of girls in acid-pink and acid-green tops was hovering near this portmanteau of manhood like coprophagous – dung-eating – gulls hovering near cows for the slugs in their dung.

A little girl in sunglasses with mint-green frontal frames, flamingo wings, standing outside her nearby, said to a little girl in a lemon and peach top who was passing:

'There are three birthday cards inside for you, Tiffany.'

'It's not my birthday.'

'It is your fucking birthday.'

And then she began chasing the other like a skua down Hyde Road, in the direction of the bus station, screaming, 'Happy Birthday to you. Happy Birthday to you.'

Flowers of the magnolia come first in Pery Square Park near the bus station, tender yellow-green leaf later.

A Traveller boy cycled by the sweet chestnut blossoms of Pery Square Park the day they found Kennedy's body, firing heaped on his handlebars.

I am forced to live in a city of Russian tattooists, murderously shaven heads, Romanian accordionists, the young in pall-bearers' clothes – this is the hemlock they've given me to drink.

The Maigue in West Limerick, as I crossed it, was like the old kettles Kennedy's ancestors used mend.

Travellers used make rings from old teaspoons and sometimes I wondered if they could make rings from the discarded Hackenberg lager cans or Mr Sheen All-Surface Polish cans beside the Metal Bridge.

I am living in the city for a year when a man who looks as if his face has been kicked in by a stallion approaches me on the street.

'I'm from Limerick City and you're from Limerick City. I know a Limerick City face. I haven't seen you there for a while. How many months did you get?'

Wooden Horse

'Took me into the gaff. Shot me in both arms. Three weeks in Tallaght Hospital. Three weeks at home recovering.'

Fifteen-year-old youth, whose body looks like a suburb of Baghdad. Sunflower-yellow hair, head shaped like one of the horses' heads in the production of *Equus* I saw, a play about a teenager who is sexually attracted to horses.

Eyes, an emerald that have been wronged, green as the horse-trampled Scheme greensward.

Septic scar on his chin.

One of the eyes of the man who shot Horsey swollen so that part of his face looked like a rancid onion.

'What happened to him?'

'He's dead.'

Horsey has a horse-and-saddle ring given to him by Joker Jewin.

Joker Jewin was born between Epsom and Croydon. Worked on the roads at Grove Park Kent with forty-six Irishmen. He was the only Englishman.

Became interested in the Republican movement.

Tattoo on his back of crossed Republican rifles, which he got in Croydon. Horse and saddle tattoo on his right arm.

Two bottles smashed in his face in a hotel in Croydon by an Orangeman. 'A nice scar for life.' Thus the name Joker as Joker in Batman who has a scar.

Rides around Tallaght in a daffodil-coloured Philip Jowett dray drawn by a monkey-coloured pony with a white square on its forehead.

Knows how to make gin-traps for rabbits and mesh traps with perch swing for crows and magpies who steal chickens' eggs or eat the young of other birds.

They have made me feel like a crow or a magpie who's been eating the blue eggs of the song thrush.

'Lie down with the dogs, wake up with fleas,' says Figroll, in a primrose-coloured hoodie jacket, 'Lie down with the pigeons and you'll wake up tumbling.'

Horsey deals drugs, often owes money.

Figroll has lonely, lonely lapis-lazuli eyes. Blue of the classroom orb of planet Earth when I was a child. In his hoodie cuirass has a head like a popping peanut.

A field mouse who has run in from the fields, a grey squirrel clasping an acorn in the Phoenix Park. The grey squirrels have reached the Grand Canal from the Phoenix Park but they who eliminated the red squirrels are in turn being coerced by escaped chipmunks.

'There's a bed and a television there,' Figroll informs me, looking at the Grand Canal. 'You could lie on the bed and watch the television.'

At fourteen or fifteen they go to the Phoenix Park at night, join the Romanian, the Polish, the Chinese boys among ilex trees, among chestnut trees and Scotch pines, among blackberry and hawthorn bushes, raise a flickering lighter. Those trackie bottoms come down. Their buttocks manifest. White ammunition.

Fifty euros each time.

Money for horses. Money for drugs.

The rabbits nibbling and the stags rutting.

'It's been going on for hundreds of years. Got stage fright at first,' says Ryaner, aged fourteen, hair the colour of New England in autumn, skin white as a squall of gulls. In an Afghan hat face like a cuckoo that comes out of a cuckoo clock.

Sometimes the guards shine magnetic cling headlights at them and they scatter into a grove of evergreen oaks.

'They go to the Phoenix Park not just for money. They want that experience.'

I'm talking to a man in a hat, T-shirt with a tropical scene – sea, sunset, palm trees – by the Grand Canal.

'Where are you from?'

'You know, where the horse hair is held.'

'Peace and love.'

Young desperado Scythians. Scythians one of the earliest people to master the art of riding. Every Scythian had at least one personal mount. They owned large herds of Mongolian ponies. Some of these sacrificed with wife, children, servants on the owner's death. Mathias, the thirteenth apostle, was saved from being eaten by them by the Apostle Andrew who'd crossed the Black Sea by express boat.

Some of the boys smoke finely rolled joints – like the cigarette sweets Rosaleen Keane in my town sold when I was a child – as they ride horses.

Palomino is a colour they say. There's a dead palomino in the fields. An abandoned piebald – all ribs.

When the horses are confiscated they're just ordinary kids, asking you to buy them smokes, asking you to buy them wine, asking you to buy them score-bag – heroin, pulling up an Iron Maiden T-shirt that has a face with skeleton's teeth, one of the teeth a miniature skull, to show you bullet wounds in their arms they got for not paying for drugs.

When the horses are gone the girls lead the boys along the canal as if they were horses.

Girls with elaborate bouffant like cross-dressers – toffee-coloured, Danny La Rue blonde, wing quiffs brushed in flamingo.

In the case of one of the boys Eak, who has a Sicilian lemon-blond turf-cut, eyes the blue of a pet parrot someone has abandoned to an Irish wilderness, a horse had previously been the girlfriend. A chestnut and white foal with chestnut measles on the white patch who would try to nuzzle his pubes the colour of carrot cake.

'Ride a cock horse to Coventry Cross
To see a fine lady on a white horse ...'
Lady Godiva rode naked through Coventry once and Peeping Tom was struck blind for looking at her when all menfolk were supposed to be indoors.

Kil, youth with butter-bath body, eyes the blue of Homer's seas, in boxers patterned with Hell flames, rides a grey Australian pony – 'a filly with a willy', he calls her – into the Square Pond

'You could put that six pack in the fridge,' Figroll comments.

Three or four year old newts returned to the Square Pond in early autumn. Crabs, lobsters here. Pike. 'Pike will bite your toes.'

Otters by the Scheme bridge.

Otters are born blind I tell Kil.

'No way.'

'Kil rode his bird in the canal once,' Figroll announces.

'I'm fishing for little, small roach', Denone, half Traveller, half Costa Rican, his mother's mother from north-west Guanacaste region – Spanish, Indian, Blacks brought to raise bananas.

A bit like a Dundee cake himself – knobs of hair, nuts of freckles.

Denone caught an otter while fishing for pike. Snapped the line. Otters have strong teeth.

Pike here – freshwater shark, perch, roach, hybrids – roach and bream mate. Tench only feed in summer. Go underwater in winter.

Denone lived for a while at Pegham Copse near Colchester where his father Pittir got a job welding gates and Pittir boxed with Three Finger Jack White at Dummers Clump in Hampshire where that Ferguson who went to Buckingham is from.

Denone learns to box at Matthew's Boxing Club in Bally-fermot and on his wall he has an advertisement for Brutal Nutrition, bare-breasted, putty-breasted ladies intermingled with boxers and the caption: 'The bad part was yesterday.'

They have a game – tea bags.

Older ones pin the younger ones on the ground and take their genitals in their mouths.

Young boys like the three puppies – mutts he called them – Tyrian purple and an incense rising inside his vertically blue-and-white striped hoodie jacket, which Figroll saved from being drowned in the Grand Canal.

'Do you want to buy one?'

Some of the genitals are too small the older boys complain.

Genitals like beetroot leaf, like sweet pea, like the catkins of the hazel tree.

Female catkins of the alder tree are hard and cone-like in autumn and maybe the small boys' penises are like that in the mouths of the older boys.

Their grandfathers used to go bird-nesting seek the buff eggs of the golden plover, the brown eggs of the lapwing, the whitish ones of the kestrel – *pocaire na gaoithe*, windfucker – and perhaps the small boys' genitals were like these eggs in the mouth.

Figroll's grandfather Bomber Sheehan was in Artane Industrial School for joy-riding at thirteen and he told Figroll about Dirty Hairy Sixpence who used to visit the school and get the boys to retrieve sixpences from down his trousers as if they were the Cleeve's Toffees or Sweet Afton cigarettes thrown towards Artane boys in Croke Park.

'Sing a Song of Sixpence
A bag full of rye
Four and twenty naughty boys,
Bak'd in a pye …'

A small boy who looks like a garden gnome in tracksuit, puts his hands down his tracksuit bottoms, showing a Jacob's Coconut Cream white belly.

Big Lips, silken-blond turf with tramlines he gets in the barber's own home on Sundays, eyes the blue of a Bible picture Nile, after his breakfast of Weetabix Chocolate Chip Minis, rides Sweet Feet, his Lucozade-coloured mare to school, tethers it to the railings, then rides it home to a lunch of a potato, a scone, a Mr Kipling Chocolate Whirl.

In the evening by the Square Pond he makes sure Sweet Feet eats white cabbage and chopped carrots as a Victorian mother would make her children eat their porridge.

'The kids think they're Tony Montano in *Scarface*.

'In this country, you got to make the money first. Then when you make the money, you get the power. Then when you get the power, then you get the women.'

Angel Lips has blonde hair in Tyrolese pigtails, heavy doll-eye makeup, green nail varnish, white plimsolls with billiard-green laces.

'You look like the fellow who robs gaffs in *Home Alone*. I love black babies. I'd love to have one. Black boys have big willies. I love Akon. He's blacker than Soulja Boy.'

Risha, aged seventeen, margarine or jaundice colour running through her hair, zebra-stripe boots, has her three-year-old son Lenzo's name in pillar tattoo on her wrist.

Lace, aged nineteen, Beaujolais Nouveau coloured hair, has her six-year-old son Ezy's name in pillar tattoo on her neck.

The government is farming out the population.

She and Ezy are going to live on Holly Estate in Tralee.

'I give him the peanut butter with jelly in it.'

Bo, aged fifteen, features that look as if they'd been fastened together by safety pins, navy leggings with a pattern of rocking horses, is pregnant by Horsey and is going to live in Limerick. Mayross she calls Moyross for beautification.

'What do you work at?'

'Bits and pieces.'

'Bits and bobs. Are you on the buildings?'

'Are you on the scratcher?' Figroll cuts in, boxers with a pattern of Santa Claus hats showing above his trackie bottoms.

'Do you want that?' Boo asks. She offers me the butt of a cigarette.

Kissy, banana-blonde hair, who wears a yellow, red, blue, green rosary around her neck, found Cleo in Palmerston Woods. A Shetland pony with a ginger mane that made him look like a Billy boy. Sores all over her body from being whipped. Suffering from bog burn – hairs falling off from the mud. Took him to Figroll who has had horses all his life.

'Sold fifteen horses this week. In the fields and upland. Turned over fifteen grand.'

Figroll bought a Clydesdale from his father. Bred near M.I. North London. 'A Clydesdale out of England.' Sold it back to him.

'Have you ever been to the Appleby Fair?' I ask Figroll.

'I heard people get raped at Appleby. Boys and girls. On the hill where they camp.

If all the money was in England and there were no Euros in Ireland England.'

If you go into Palmerston Woods bring a stick in case a badger attacks you. If he attacks break the stick because he'll think that's a bone breaking. The badger will attack you until a bone in the ankle breaks.

Figroll was camping by Blessington Lake once. There was an American pit bulldog on a leash there. A badger attacked Figroll. He threw a stick at it.

A miniature Jack Russell will shake a rat and break its neck if he catches it. But the badger will kill a Jack Russell.

Smelly John from Edmonton, a tomato-coloured laceration under his right eye, has half a black Border collie called Loo, blind in one eye, and a Santa Claus Pomeranian called Judge, who can combat badgers.

Twelve badgers live in Palmerston Woods and have built tunnels of escape there. I feel like them.

'You'd be better off in Jail,' says Smelly John from Edmonton looking towards Wheatfield Prison where he spent time staging American pit bulldog fights, 'Three square meals a day. Television. Snooker. Training courses. They treat you well if you belong to an illegal organization. Catholic or Protestant. There are Orangemen in the south. There are Orangemen all over the south.

There was a fellow there with the Orange lily and 1690 on his leg.'

'How's your love life?'

In winter twilight, a cilium of very yellow reed canary grass by the canal, Figroll suddenly pulls down his trackie bottoms.

'Is there a bruise on me arse?'

Donkey Lips, a jack rabbit in a scarlet Éire-Ireland T-shirt 2011, lights up the intense orifice with the light of his mobile phone, buttocks like the pronunciations on the heron's neck.

Dirck van Baburen couldn't have done better.

On a May evening when purple lilac is mixed with the hawthorn blossom, Figroll suddenly demonstrates his penis as if it was a machine.

His hair Easter chick yellow and barley, but an arc of a penis above eclipsed water-rat coloured pubes.

'Doesn't Figroll have a very big prick?' asks Tooler admiringly, eyes blue as Croagh Patrick, protean, early adolescent features, changed since autumn when his hair looked like a wren's nest stomped on his head, and he wore a wild bear colour anorak.

A baby bear escaped from Dublin Zoo sixteen years ago and came to the Square Pond.

Figroll looks like one of the sons of Laocoön in the sculptural group that influenced Michelangelo, constrictor sea serpent from the Greek camp on the island of Tenedos wound about date-cluster genitals.

Laocoön was a priest of Troy who broke his vow of celibacy by begetting Antiphantes and Thymbraeus and was punished for both.

Wooden horse built by Epeius, the master carpenter, so the Greeks could gain access to Troy.

Smithfield – cattle, hay market since 1664. Horses sold here since late 1800s. Everything sold here – ferrets, rats.

I'd seen the turnover in horses, the sudden rejection of paramour horses, the sallying to Smithfield Square that had been lined with farmyards until recently, to buy a new horse or exchange a horse with fifty euros in the difference.

'He doesn't sleep with his Mum and Dad. He's got a girlfriend. He fancies me. But he fancies you the same.'

Three Romany girls near me at Smithfield Market early March.

One in poinsettia-red mini dress.

One with miniature melon picture hat as hair ornament.

One in denim hot pants with bib, and reflector-yellow high heels.

One of the girl's father comes from England to sell rope harnesses here but his mother has settled in Kilmacthomas in County Waterford.

The girl's bodies have creosote oil on them used for railway sleepers – boards with horizontally go across railway tracks – used for the wooden engine of the Bouncy Castle Rodeo Bull, the young, city-centre based manager I'm talking to, horse at side, cartoon cowboy on it, which he brought to Appleby Fair, which he brought to the Horse Fair in the town I'm from, when the left arm of a youth – a koala bear, a brindled boxer dog, a tortoise-shell butterfly in a black, white fur, trimmed hoodie jacket – is slashed with a machete nearby.

'Sliced like an orange by a sword,' Tooler, whom I meet shortly afterwards, describes it.

Shots are fired from a makeshift gun, causing mayhem – lost purses, stolen horses – and a horse stampede, which looks like one of Michael Cimino's panoramas of the Wyoming Johndon War of the 1890s.

'Doesn't he have big balls?'

Tooler's older brother Fluffy, eyes the blue of a cornflower, who has run away from home, in a jacket with a Native American horse at the back of it, pulls back the tail of a chestnut Newforest pony bought at Smithfield and walked home along the Grand Canal that Sunday when blows were rained with tyre irons.

'Indiana Jones,' he cries, riding away on the Newforest pony, recalling Indiana Jones riding a rhinoceros while chasing a truck in Africa.

'Did you sell any horses in Smithfield?' I ask Baz, a boy whose hair in autumn was chick-feather light dun. Now it's turtle coloured. It grows on his head like a clump of chives from an old teapot. But his eyes are still the eyes of babyhood.

'No, I sold donkeys.'

The Jerusalem two-stroke Figroll calls a donkey.

Baz has a little donkey, Amy, from County Mayo, who looks as if snow has fallen on her and some of it turned to slush.

'You could get Channel 4 on those ears,' extols Figroll.

In 1600 Cheapside vintner William Banks' bay gelding Marocco, shoed in silver, known to Shakespeare, Ben Jonson, Sir Walter Raleigh, Dekker, Rowley, Middleton, climbed to the top of Saint Paul's Cathedral, to the applause of braying donkeys.

Donkey Lips' eyes are a piñata – a children's party he doesn't want me to come to. When I ask the colour of his eyes and try to look at them he scrunches up his face like a scrolled baby's napkin.

'That's a weird question for these parts. Would you ask the Limerick boys what's the colour of their eyes?'

'I had to stop Donkey Lips from knifing you for asking the colour of his eyes,' Figroll warns me later.

Limerick boys …

When you've lived in a place for thirteen years, and you're suddenly driven out – the riverine haw, the sloes, the rosehips you miss, the riverside and companionable Travellers' horses.

The piebald horses had snowdrop-white patches. Snowdrops the comfrey that came to the Shannon meadows in May was called.

The loss of a child is a terrible thing; the loss of children (plural) is even more terrible. The loss of a community of children is devastating.

In exile though you remember your friends, their faces …

Remembering them, their kindness, remembering the river, gives you fortitude and resolve …

Laocoön and Cassandra, priest and priestess of Troy, gave their oracles and were not believed.

Laocoön tried to set the wooden horse on fire.

He threw a spear at it.

A few days after that Sunday at Smithfield someone comes to the Square Pond and shoots Big Lips' mare Sweet Feet in the head just as she is about to have a foal. Foal comes out anyway and Big Lips starts hand-feeding it.

It is like the story of Jane Seymour and Edward VI.

'King Henry, King Henry, I know you to be:
Pray cut my side open and find my baby.'

Then the Pound, in apparent retaliation for the violence of a Traveller family who got to a Traveller family they were feuding with, in a wooden horse, swoops.

Eighteen horses and four donkeys driven down fields to field owned by NAMA. National Asset Management Agency.

Horsey's stallion Flash hides in the osiers and escapes.

Five days to claim them. They are kept twenty-eight days. 'Pound said it all cost thirty-eight grand.'

Figroll, Horsey, Kil, Fluffy, Tooler, Big Lips, Donkey Lips, Denone, Eak go to the Council Offices in Tallaght to plead, led by Skaf, a youth in his twenties, woollen hat making his eyes look troglodyte, buried. But it's like chasing the tooth fairy. Figroll's mother, whose medication for migraine is wearing the calcium on her teeth, rings up. The horses and donkeys are dead.

Figroll tells me that the horses from the Traveller site at Fonthill Road – where a Traveller man with hair dyed the red of Danny Kaye had asked me one day: 'Did you get married yet?' – to Kinnegad, County Westmeath, put down, burned in the Cement factory.

'They give horse meat to feed tigers in the zoo, to dog food factories, they give the dead horses to glue factories.'

Two youths from Ballymun sit on the edge of the almost deserted Smithfield plaza towards the end of the fair, like herons waiting in unison by the Grand Canal. Horses that don't have a microchip are confiscated at Smithfield now, so there is a samizdat horse fair on the top of Chapelizod Hill.

'I'll give you a thousand euros now and the rest in Coolock.'

Someone rings up the Joe Duffy Show to say the Scheme boys were cruel to horses and deserved the horses and donkeys being taken. The boys are convinced it was me. Identical voice.

'Didn't you ring up the Joe Duffy Show and say we were cruelty to horses?' Figroll accuses.

'Two English people went to Coolock and asked to see the horses. Then the Pound came.'

Surrounded by boys, some like the wolf of Gubbio with a stud in its ear, some with a caduceus — staff of Mercury — by a torched Go-Kart, I am made to feel like Gypo Nolan in John Ford's film, who is taunted by a prostitute during the War of Independence because he doesn't have the fare to the USA, accepts a British award leading to the arrest of his friend Frankie McPhillip, revealing Frankie's where-abouts, seeks expiation in Dublin's churches, tried in secret by his former comrades, shot.

It was no use denying I'd rung up the Joe Duffy Show. I had to accept it though it wasn't true, and go through a period of vilification.

'Paedo. Faggot. Rat. You egg. You fuel. You did the monkey. What's the colour of your eyes? I'll buy you a pair of socks.'

Figroll gets a replacement horse, a skewbald from the Leitrim mountains with white fur like a goose's feathers.

'A psycho horse.'

'He's a spirit. Mad as a brush. Mad as a fork. Mad as a spoon.'

I feel like that horse, on the ground by the Square Pond, head tethered by many ropes held by the youths, beaten on the face with a fleecey butter-green poplar bough by Figroll until the blood runs from his face and mouth, thought to have expired, rising, standing, anticipating further blows.

Banger, a Chihuahua of a boy, hair as black as the black of a chess-board, eyebrows like black sickle moons, cherry-cordial lips, cheekbones scalloped like a holy-water font, runs excitedly in the middle of this entertainment as a moorhen hobbles in the fields.

Banger has two bracelets of miniature ikons, one large, one smaller, dominant ikon in the large one that of a Christ who looks like Tony Montano in *Scarface*.

'Where did you get the bracelet?'

'In Lourdes.'

'When were you in Lourdes?'

'I wasn't. My nanny was. Where's yours?'

Figroll has two similar bracelets. One a gypsy woman had given him in town. 'She only gives them to special people.' One the Leitrim owner of the skewbald had given him for luck.

In identical magenta tracksuits, two girls smoke cigarettes on the gate, but with the look of Martha and Abby Brewster, the two spinster aunts in *Arsenic and old Lace*, before they poison one of their gentlemen victims with elderberry wine laced with arsenic, strychnine, cyanide.

Suddenly one of them screams.

'He did a shit.'

Horsey emerges from behind the hawthorn bushes, carrying a stick with excrement at the end, and goes in the direction of the girls. Excrement gets on the white jackets he's carrying. He looks to the Grand Canal for a solution.

The Pound strike again, confiscating the Leitrim skewbald, and that is the finish for me. 'You were a spy from the SPCA.'

Fluffy in a hoodie jacket patterned with skulls tries to tether my bicycle to an elder tree. Figroll simultaneously tries to wrest the bicycle from me.

'I was fond of you,' I plead.

I want to say you and the other boys came into my life in a wooden horse.

I wanted to say I'd known a wooden horse since childhood. The Horse Fair in my town was a wooden horse in which people who were different came.

Thomas Omer started building the Grand Canal in 1757. One of his houses is by the twelfth lock with deadly nightshade on the other side of the canal. The twelfth lock was built too narrow on the Dublin side. It had to be widened. The mares and foals among the ragwort by the twelfth lock know not to eat it because of its poisonous juices.

The Grand Canal was built with gunpowder, picks, shovels, candles.

Horses used draw barges by the canal. That's why the boys claimed in Tallaght Council Offices they had a right to own horses.

'Have you ever heard the expression "Keep on the straight and the narrow"?' Kil asked me one day, in Bermudas patterned with Brazil nuts, 'It comes from the Grand Canal. The long barges were pulled by a horse on a straight and narrow path. The path had to be straight and narrow to keep the tension of the barge'

Getting across the Bog of Allen took five years.

They got to Daingean – Philipstown after Queen Mary's Spanish husband ('My marriage is my own affair.') – where there was another reformatory school. I knew someone who was turned barefoot out of it.

Then the canal extended to Shannon Harbour. An extension beyond the Shannon to the town I'm from.

There was a Guinness depot there. Coffee Bradley, a Somme veteran, came down the Grand Canal in a Guinness barge, as King of the Horse Fair, like Elizabeth I sailing down the River Effra to visit Sir Walter Raleigh at Raleigh Hall, who mentioned Banks' horse Marocca in his *History of the World*.

Redser Lardon's mother used to walk an armada of cocker spaniels, Chinese pug dogs, Welsh corgis around town. She usually wore an olive-and-beige scarf at her neck. They lived in a Regency town house with moss-coloured door, lead lights over door, foot scraper by door.

He suffered from Down Syndrome.

When I used be hitchhiking outside town, close to the Church of Our Lady of Lourdes, he'd stop and talk. Always wore a belted great coat. Strawey cockscomb. Would shuffle and snort with laughter. Sometimes carried *Eagle* and *Beano* comics and would engage you in conversation about Dan Dare or Walter the Softy. Inference was that I was a bit of Walter the Softy.

'What goes around, comes around,' he'd say.

When his mother died he drowned himself in the Grand Canal.

'I liked you too,' Figroll says – he's in a squirrel-coloured hoodie jacket, 'but I think there's something weird about you.

What makes you wet the bed? Are you a steamer? Will you steam with me? I'm fast on bald men. I went with Baldy Paddy Beatley.'

Baldy Paddy Beatley let four dogs go wild in the fields.

A lurcher (greyhound/deerhound), face of a Patterdale.

Whippy – cross Labrador, Staffordshire terrier, with carrion skin.

Greyhound/Irish deerhound/Saluki (Arab hunting dog), bit of Bedlington.

A dog he called a lurcher but with its fur looked like soaked breadcrumbs.

'If they attack you you put your finger up their arse,' Tooler had advised me.

'He was bareback.'

Naked, Baldy Paddy Beatley had crow-coloured hairs all over his body, his body looked like a potato field covered with crows.

'Baldy Paddy Beatley used box. His favourite punch was backhand. I was a whippet he said. I'm not eighteen anymore. I've no fucking teeth.

He said he boxed with two Knackers from Mullingar who went on to the Olympic Games. The Knackers in Mullingar stand fifty feet apart from one another and throw things at one another he said.'

Figroll flings an empty Perlenbacher bottle at me.

'Baldy Paddy Beatley has his woolly hat pulled over his eyes. Like a real paedo. Why don't you pull your hat over your eyes?'

'It's either in you or it isn't. It's a tradition. The horses are more like dogs. Come to the door in this weather.' The snowmen in the Scheme look more like crazy banshees than snowmen. 'They come home. The scatter-brained ones won't.'

Sometimes when I wake up at night or can't sleep it's as if a horse comes to the door. A horse that's been put down. A youth's face like one of the ghosts of horses on the walls of Trois Frères. An asymmetrical henna-coloured horse like one of the horses on the walls of Lascaux. The prehistoric white horse carved on top of the Berkshire Downs at Uffington. The horse presented as gift by King Oswin that Saint Aidan of Lindisfarne, whose bones were brought back to Galway by his successor Colman, immediately gave to a poor man.

Near Lindisfarne in Northumberland there's a poppy field.

An autobiography-writing horse like the disabled Anna Sewell's Black Beauty.

'Boys you see think a horse is like a steam engine or a thrashing machine, and can go as long and as fast as they please; they never think that a pony can get tired, or have feelings.'

William Banks' gelding Marocco who was possibly burned by the Inquisition with his master in Rome or Lisbon.

The kissing and counting mare Samuel Pepys saw at Bartholomew Fair on a September day on which he was later invited by a wench to her room in Shoe Lane.

The horse on which the actor Edmund Keane, as a boy, dressed as a monkey, used do somersaults on at Bartholomew Fair and fell off, damaging both legs.

Begun in the early Middle Ages Bartholomew Fair in West Smithfield in London – Ruffians Hall – where men fought with sword and buckler for twelve pence, was suppressed by the Victorians on the grounds of debauchery.

'... it causeth swearing, it causeth swaggering, it causeth snuffling and snarling, and now and then a hurt ... Hide, and be hidden; ride and be ridden, says the vapour of experience ...'

When Ben Jonson's work failed elsewhere he turned to the expensive, private theatres where only young boys acted.

A wooden horse comes to my door – a youth in a hoodie jacket with hair over his mouth the colour of biblical dates who turned into a wooden horse.

Wreathes by the Grand Canal change from white to electric blue, from poly-colours to white and scarlet, scarlet of blood, scarlet of poinsettia wreathes of New Orleans.

A girl with geyser hair-style, crimson on top, cerulean cord around her hair, kneels by the Grand Canal and weeps for her brother as the sun sets.

I take her hand.

'It was just a stupid accident.'

'I've suffered too,' I tell her. 'I know what it's like.'

'There are no cash machines in graveyards,' says Mad Mickey Teeling, 'Spend what you have now.'

Mad Mickey Teeling wears a cap covered in badges – Martin Doherty killed Ardoyne Belfast, James Larkin, James Connolly, Che Guevara, nine Hunger Strikers ('one missing,' he apologizes), the Irish colours and also a 1960 halfpenny on it.

He has a Central Asia shepherd dog called Eric.

'You get ten years for robbing a shop,' he complains, 'but paedophiles only get two.

The priest who baptized me and married my parents molested children.'

The horses were their imagination, the horses narratives, the horses were anthropoid like Dumbo the flying elephant and his one friend Timothy Mouse, or like Anna Sewell's Black Beauty, Ginger, Merrylegs.

'Can you remember Black Beauty's friend's name?' Figroll asked me one day.

He hadn't read the book but he'd seen the film where Black Beauty narrated his story voice-over.

'Ginger? Merrylegs?'

Hash dipped on acid, hash with melted-down glass dipped in diesel, Kepplers cider, house music.

Monksfield after ten when the off-licences close, the guards coming looking for them.

Dumbo was taunted by the other elephants because he had big ears. Mrs Jumbo, his mother, was locked up as a mad woman for defending her child. Dumbo was forced to be a circus clown who has to fall into a vat of pie filling. With the help of his friend Timothy Mouse and some crows Dumbo discovered his ability to fly because of his big ears and he became a circus celebrity.

There was a circus in the field opposite the Jensen Hotel and Shell garage.

They wanted Mad Mickey Teeling's Central Asian shepherd dog when he brought it to the circus grounds.

'He can be a cunt. You'd want to see the hiding I gave him,' he told them to put them off.

A man with a belly like a plum pudding with cream on top, asked the boys to distribute circus leaflets with the motorbike globe of death on them, and when their task was done, as the circus lights turned from yellow to red to aquamarine to purple, as the jungle drums beat within the tent, had sex with some of them.

Figroll smoked three joints one morning, took twenty-four-hour pills, drank a bottle of Huzzar vodka, stole a scarlet, white and yellow Honda CO 21.

'A horse must have jumped on it.'

Set it on fore in Brennan's Field.

'I was on a buzz. I pissed on my mobile. You could see the piss on the screen.'

In Ireland in the nineteenth-century it was believed that the song-thrush built its nest cup of leaves and twigs, lined with mud, low in trees and bushes so the fairies in their houses in the grass could enjoy their music. But this did not prevent Figroll from telling a song thrush in Brennan's Field 'Shut your fucking mouth.'

'Someone snitched on me. I was crying when I got to the police station. It takes a big man to say sorry and Figroll says sorry.'

Pinocchio's nose grew longer when he lied. The moustaches or lip growth on boys in Oberstown Boys Centre where Figroll was sent told you they'd committed a crime. Figroll joined the boys with faces pale as mousetrap cheese, youths you would formerly see at Smithfield Horse Fair; anxious to sell horses, with a half-starved look, knifed cheeks.

'Now farewell to the Faire ...'

City of exile, city of loneliness.

I live in a world without stories. Without friends.

Diogenes of Greece walked the street with a lighted candle looking for a human being.

I feel like him.

Seven doomed horses and a donkey from Mayo sequestering themselves under the trees, at different angles from one another, nosing one another.

There's something very human about horses.

They tried to stop my heart the way they stop horses' hearts, giving them an injection.

'Love is boat that swim for most,' says Bo, in a leopard-spot top with bare midriff, before she leaves for Moyross, Limerick, holding a baby like a marshmallow hedgehog in a fluffy jacket.

'What leave ye to your father, King Henry, my son?

The keys of old Ireland, and all that's therein ...'

Brimstone Butterfly

Zapamtite. Remember. Arriving in Zagreb on a freezing November evening. Like Prague – subdued city lights, the coloured ones at intervals from one another, like lighthouses, a peculiar kind of pharos.

Posters all along the airport route for Lenny Kravitz who sang once for the California Boys' Choir.

I give a girl in a pinafore patterned with steam-irons fifty Kuna for twenty-nine Kuna groceries in a shop on Palmotićeva. Makes to return twenty kuna change but swiftly puts it back in the till.

When I manage to argue it back I feel like the woman who found the lost silver coin and rejoiced.

Dimitris – musclé like Christiano Ronaldo, mermaid's-tail green eyes, in a T-shirt with a sad Cherokee chief on it, under a three-dimensional photograph of elephants, one moment a solitary elephant, the next at a slightly different angle an elephant with a baby elephant, in a flat by the Royal Canal in Dublin – had told me the joke. The Demon arrives in Stockholm and causes havoc. He arrives in Berlin and there is chaos in Germany. On arrival at Zagreb Airport he immediately screams: 'The Croatians have robbed my suitcase!'

At Zagreb Airport Petar, born year of Vukovar massacre in Daruvar, a Titan with a bottle-nose dolphin face who plays basketball and soccer in St Louis now, had stood on front of the candle.

Small lights in red glass along the edges of boulevards, arrangements of these lights in green spaces.

Zapamtite. Remember.

A sixteen-year-old boy had been among the two hundred and sixty people taken from Vukovar Hospital who were massacred near the village of Ovčara, bodies dumped in a wooded ravine.

'I first learned to ride a motorcycle,' Dimitris told me, 'Then I stole my aunt's car when I was thirteen and learned to drive. Two years later drove my aunt's car in the war.'

'To a cruel war I sent him, from whence he return'd his brows bound with oak.'

Dimitris came back from war with a tattoo on his leg of Japanese Samurai Miyamoto Musashi, in Japanese pantaloons and hose with a top of Mount Fuji pattern, killing an opponent with a bokken – a staff.

Leontis had done the tattoo.

Hair like mashed bananas and eyes the colour of a crown of thorns that had verdigris.

'Keep it quiet.'

Dogs of War. Christopher Walken mercenaries.

Bear goulash and hog goulash between sneak attacks.

At seventeen they entered an eighty-year-old Serbian woman's house near Vukovar. Her scarf patterned with butterflies hovering over garden flowers. Dimitris and another youth went upstairs.

Leontis enters her sitting-room that had a Mr and Mrs Duck in it, he in blue dungarees, chocolate polka-dot scarf, she in blue bib dress not unlike her husband's outfit.

Old hogs going blind run at everything.

She threw a grenade that killed Leontis beyond recognition.

'We put her on the stick,' said Dimitris sipping liquorice liqueur – *Licor a la Sambuca* – as his budgie Hannibal and his canary Lecter, called after Dr Hannibal 'The cannibal' Lecter in *The Silence of the Lambs*, chirruped in their cage.

Impaled her.

This was a Partisan method of revenge immediately after the war.

Pointed wooden pole greased with oil, forced into the anus, pushed through until it emerged around collar bone, wide end of the stick placed in a hole in the ground, and the victim hoisted for all to see.

'Toblerone, Turkish Delight, weed helps me with post-traumatic stress syndrome. And she does.'

Zyna, Dimtris's girlfriend, went to her job in a Dublin bakery with her honey-blonde hair like a cluster-bomb explosion, black boa, shoulder bag like a laminated magpie's or wren's nest, face the colour of a Steve Reeves movie – *Romolo e Remo* maybe – jackboots that Kaiser Wilhelm's favourite Count Philip zu Eulenberg, banished for his proclivities, might have worn.

Beech, lime, birch, maple leaves, the ground outside Alojzije Stepinac's Cathedral of the Assumption of the Blessed Virgin Mary, the verdure by the cathedral, covered with the leaves of a Japanese pagoda tree, like gold coins, riches you have saved up.

Smell of chrysanthemums, candytuft, mistletoe, dried figs from Dolac market.

A nun in black-and-white veil comes down Skalinska – a wynd near the cathedral.

The fragile Alojzije Stepinac welcomed and had close links with Ante Pavelić's Nazi satellite Independent State of Croatia, many against him, many for him, his strongest supporters the Jews who know of the assistance he gave to Croatia's Jews. It is widely believed that the body that lies in the cathedral was poisoned by Communist agents.

'My grandparents were Ustaše. The People who rise,' Dimitris had told me, 'They said times were good then. The old people said times were good then.'

From childhood Croatians hear how Saint Nikolo Tavelić was cut to pieces by the Moslems in Palestine in 1391.

As we drank Turkish mocca coffee from Croatia I had it recounted: Poles thrown over cliffs; knives, saws, hammers, wheatsheaf cutters, machetes, piano wire, wooden mallets, clubs, rifle butts, bayonets as a method of death; the crane gallows by the River Sava at Jasenovac Concentration Camp the winter before final defeat, bodies slashed and throats slit before being flung in the current; throat-slitting competitions; heads sawn off; children's heads severed and thrown on mothers laps; children's heads dashed against schools-walls; arms and legs cut off, eyes, tongues, hearts cut out, breasts severed; not to mention death by gas, by fire as happened to those locked inside Glina Orthodox Church (this the reason for a letter from Stepinac to Pavelić); eyes and human organs gloatingly displayed in the cafés of Tkalčićeva in Zagreb.

'Pavelić escaped to Argentina, was shot in Buenos Aires, died in Madrid and there's a gold tomb for him there.'

Dimitris's mother's grandfather had been a lieutenant in Treblinka, executed after the war.

His grandfather received toxic barrels of waste from the Soviet Union. Most people had car licences for certain days. He had a car licence for all days. He opened one of the barrels and his organs became disarrayed. He died in one week. Dimitris's father, who was imprisoned for going to Mass, was near one of the barrels and got an ulcer.

Zyna's grandmother – her mother's mother – a Russian, was put in Dachau.

'You'll be sent to the cells,' I was warned.

Packing your belongings into boxes, sacks, possible imprisonment. Who will collect the boxes and sacks? Who will collect the life, the existence?

A Jewish woman has recently managed to reclaim her family heirloom of Gustave Klimt paintings stolen by the Nazis and you remember in gold Jewish women taken to concentration camps in fur coats, wearing excess jewellery, wearing their jewellery so it could be saved. Jewish people rounded up at a theatre in Amsterdam, Hollandse Schouwburg, a stop for a day before the train to Westerbork, then farther east.

After a front-page Sunday tabloid article my mountain bicycle is grabbed outside my basement bedsit. I find it wrecked on the other side of the eighteenth-century building, white splashes from the carrion crows nesting above all over the place, as if they were engaging in amateur painting.

Frame kicked in. Two wheels mercilessly buckled. Brake wires pulled out. More damage done by stomping on it, by a man whose face looks like a plate of rashers. I am thrown on the ground and kicked like a Kerry football. A Stella Artois bottle is thrown at me.

'The newspapers never lie,' declare his girlfriend in a diamante halter top, matching hot pants, her body like a pudding stuffed into this attire and supported by stars-and-stripes block high heels.

A Japanese Spitz dog is watching this from afar. 'Get back on your lead at once,' a lady in a summer dress with lotus flowers and South Sea sunsets on it says to him and walks off with him.

A crowd comes and bangs on my door some nights later. 'Where's the paedophile?' Like a lynch mob in Alabama. Do they intend to hang me from a lime tree in the Belfry?

A mug with vintage cars and car horns is thrown through my window. I keep very silent and they leave.

Romanians greet me cordially. Offering sweet anadems – a watch with enamelled dial, crystal surround, gold-plated, for sale outside Lidl.

A man who used drink with Pecker Dunne, author of 'Sullivan's John', in Jet Carroll's in Listowel, drives me across the Curragh – a heroic landscape – playing Margo – 'West of the Old River Shannon' and Mike Denver – 'I Want to Be in Ireland for the Summer'.

Pecker Dunne, whose grandfather Bernie used to busk at the Country Shop Café in Dublin, claimed he wrote 'Sullivan's John' when he was eleven.

A farmer's son Johnny Sullivan fell in love with a Traveller girl at Pecker Dunne's site in Kilrush, County Clare, and ran away with her. Off to England where he started a tarmac and trucking business. The song has him carrying a Traveller's box of tools.

In a glory-hole by the Royal Canal with a view of Mountjoy Jail I find a traumatized Brimstone butterfly – yellow with orange spots – who has stowed away among images wrapped in cotton teacloths my mother sent me when I lived in Limerick – images numerously scrutinized, even my Madonnas, as possible pornography, Antoine-Denis Chaudet's *Cupid and the Butterfly* from the Louvre, posthumously finished by Pierre Cartellier, naked crouching teenage boy with pigeon wings feeding a butterfly on a plinth, eliciting even leers because of his committed buttocks.

In 1702 there'd been the Brimstone butterfly fraud when Brimstone butterflies had been painted with eyespots and declared a new species.

I release the butterfly in the direction of Mountjoy Jail.

'It's a terrible thing Mountjoy,' a youth by the Grand Canal, with a turf cut that looks as if it's been done by a lawnmower, face the red of someone who's just been up and down the Sugarloaf, eyes like Badlands fires, yellow and emerald Manchester United protest scarf around his neck, tells me.

'Grown men using a bucket for urinating as a toilet. Mountjoy is terrible. You light a cigarette on a bunk in the middle of the night and you see cockroaches. The cockroaches. The cockroaches have been there since it was built.'

When I was first put in Mountjoy in the middle of the night it was the caravan cell. Four bunk beds. Eight people, four sleep on the floor. Travellers thrown in there a lot.

Young Travellers go on suicide watch. Twenty-three-hour lock down, padded cells.

'I was in jail. Zagreb. Llubljana. Italy.' Dimitris wears a chocolate-coloured T-shirt with a deranged Mr T from *The A-Team* on it.

When they first moved into this flat they were robbed – socks, toilet paper, even things in the fridge were stolen.

Their fridge magnet shows four completely covered Moslem women and a small boy with the word 'Mom' in a dialogue bubble.

Dimitris was shot in left foot in Milan, stabbed on right side Via Roma, Rijeka – Fiume – which Gabriele D'Annunzio and three hundred supporters occupied in 1919 and which he ruled as dictator until December 1920.

Their fathers killed in the war, children start sniffing glue by the canal theatre.

One of them, a boxer, beat people up and threw them in the canal.

Ships travelling to Rijeka from the South throw food into the sea and sharks follow — *modruy* Zyna calls them — they come into the archipelago. Then they get trapped because of shallow water.

Helicopters — choppers for Dimitris — shoot when they see a shark's tail in summer.

Post-traumatic stress syndrome.

After the war — the clean ups in Moslem Bosnia — life is a collage. Berlin, Munich, Stockholm, Amsterdam, Rome, Palermo, Dublin.

Armed robbery — jail.

He stole Marshal Tito's watch from a museum in Zagreb and sold it to a Jewish man in Piazza Goldone Trieste.

Hid on Cres Island for a while before being sent to jail.

Then armed robbery again. International journeys ending in Palermo.

Return. Jail.

Organized crime. He and Zyna manage to get to Dublin the year a design of a woman with plentiful hair playing a harp that Ivan Meštrović submitted for the coins of the Irish Free State in 1927, but too late for consideration, is finally used on a commemorative coin.

Before he left he started kicking a Jewish youth with whom he'd had an argument on the ground and the youth clung to Zyna's boots.

He didn't know why he did it.

Ustaše?

Black Legion? The Nazis got the uniforms for them.

Didn't I know of Ivica Čuljak? Panonski after the Roman Pannonia Inferior. Painter. Poet. Actor. Punk singer. From Vinkcovci near Vukovar — Chicago of Yugoslavia.

Mental Casualty. How the Punk Defended Croatia.

Five seconds after the concert begins in Maksimir Stadium in Zagreb riot squad called in. Used cut himself during performances so he looked like a mutilated ant. Twelve years for killing a man in self-defence. Spent time in a mental institution near Zagreb. Wore the uniform of the Croatian National Guard when war started. Joined the army to defend his mother. Turned up in a Belgrade nightclub during the war. Dimitris says that because of his enthusiasm with hatchet and chainsaw in combat he was shot in his bunker by the Croatian army.

And even just now Marko Perković and his group Thompson who sing songs in praise of Ustaše Croatia get 60,000 people in Zagreb, many wearing Ustaše insignia.

What does she think of Alojzije Stepinac I ask Zyna? She's wearing a T-shirt with a mannequin cat's face on it.

'He was a good man.'

The world's borders changed. Old acquaintances faded into the night like the ghosts of yesteryear. Your only friends a Croatian couple. He involved in clean-up operations in Bosnian villages at fifteen. From Bosnian villages to Plunkett Tower in Ballymun.

Wars have brought us together.

Arriving in Dublin Dimitris and Zyna initially lived in the only occupied tower in Ballymun, Plunkett Tower.

Towers at Silloge and Shangan were waiting to be destroyed. They burnt rubbish under them.

At the reception youths, scamgany, skaggy boys, some on drugs, would ask for money, would ask for sweets.

'Arriving in a new place you must always get to know the social bottom first.'

Daso, aged eighteen, Sonic the Hedgehog hairstyle, injected himself.

Water bubble in syringe went through his body as blood clot to his heart and killed him.

Rozzer, aged fifteen, hoodlum in hoodie look — took too much methadone, went home, got sick in his sleep, choked on his own vomit.

While they were there some boys stole six rabbits, set a deaf pit bull terrier on them in Coultry Park, mutilated the rabbits with their own hands.

Dimitris and Zyna threw their passports into a fire under a tower at Silloge.

As a fugitive the only job Dimitris could get was as a gravedigger from County Antrim.

There he worked with Robo, a gravedigger from County Antrim. Inebriated pike expression, long face, flinted features.

Robo's grandmother – his father's mother – had ninety-three grandchildren. Mother Shiggins.

Robo's uncle used drive Robo around Antrim on a Bill Wright pot cart. Mending pots and pans on the way. They'd go to small fairs. Sleep under the cart.

Robo's uncle's house was a shed. Donkey in the shed too.

He raised chunky chickens for Christmas. Stole wood from building sites. Gathered fallen trees with Robo's help. Sold them as logs for Christmas. He used a bow saw.

Some of the Shiggins beat the Lambeg Drum at two Orange gatherings each year in Tennessee.

Robo came South to see the site of the battle of the Boyne and became a grave-digger, often exposing the Eve with very nude breasts on his back from Sailor Bill in Portrush.

'He was a sailor. Did tattoos in Portrush and Colraine. His son Bruce carried on the business.'

Nuns had babies, threw the babies into lime, he informed Dimitris.

Digging seven feet deep one day Dimitris broke a coffin and stepped in yellow jelly.

A mother asked him to put a cross on a three-month-old baby's neck. He opened the coffin and the head fell off and he had to pick up the head.

Memories of Second World War Ustaše massacres of Serb children.

The mother started spitting at him. The priest was alien to him Dimitris said.

'On my twenty-eighth birthday I buried five babies.'

'Arriving in a new place you must get to know the social bottom first.'

Arriving at the house by the Royal Canal Dimitris and Zyna immediately got to know Mosher and Peggy's Leg who drank Brasserie beer by Tesco's.

Eyes swallowed in Mosher's face the way insects are swallowed in the pitcher plant that grows in Roscommon and Westmeath, leaving an echo of deep-sea blue, youngish face that has Patriarch's scrolls.

Peggy's Leg wears a rainbow-striped woollen hat and her hair is the colour of Marie Antoinette's wig.

'You meet the nicest people in the Joy,' Mosher tells me, 'The ones outside should be inside and the ones inside should be outside.

Some get out and are in again on a running charge after a week. They're used to it. It's a way of life. The way it is, you get fed. It's cheaper to be inside.

I've lived on the streets for years and I know everyone. If you're with me you're alright.

'I've been a landlord for twenty-five years and every nutcase in Ireland has passed through my hands,' the landlord, a man from Carlow with a face the colour of marmalade, says.

The house we live in is peaceful now but Dimitris and Zyna tell me about some of its recent occupants.

A man from Kazakhstan who thought Moslems were after him and going to bomb him and who set the curtains and mattress on fire and threw the mattress on fire outside on the landing.

A man who thought Dimitris and Zyna were spies and that Tesco's was a spy ring.

A Bosnian Moslem who was always banging drawers, shelves, doors.

A woman from Moldova with three children, including an ice-blond, almost narcissus-haired boy. 'I am divorce-ed.'

Kookie arrived with a bottle of Scottish sparkling water and nothing else.

Three times she'd run away from a mental hospital.

She used wrap her body in tinfoil, put clothes over tinfoil, then don a tinfoil headdress, sleep in the hall in this apparel. Thought there were a million people in her room.

Once went naked to Tesco's except for bits of tinfoil wrapped around her, many of which fell off.

'She was a phrenic,' Dimitris whispers.

'I have a friend. Painter.'

Age of consent is fourteen in Croatia but Slavko was accused of spiking a seventeen-year-old boy with drugs and drink and then having sex with him.

Due at prison hospital with his solicitor – his 'brief' (Dimitris uses a word he learnt from Mosher), Dimitris picked him up.

The escape route was florid. Naum in Bosnia. Montenegro. Serbia. Kosova.

Going south to Albania, to keep the map, the atlas of desire alive.

Dimitris got Slavko to safety in Tirana, Albania.

Dimitris picks up a photograph from over the fireplaces of Slavko swimming with a fifteen-year-old Albanian boy in Lake Ohrid, Macedonia, Slavko in briefs with a jabberwocky pattern, blue, yellow, red, the boy who has a pencil-line moustache in sailor-stripe jersey briefs with a red rim.

'There are twenty Croatian mercenaries in Dublin,' Dimitris tells me. If ever I need help.

Croatian mercenaries in Burma communicate video footage to Dimitris's computer of people being executed in Burma.

A Pakistani couple with a child move into one of the unoccupied flats and soon there are broken Chivas Regal bottles all over the back. The council won't take the rubbish because of bottles in it and rubbish bags accumulate and one evening I come home and find that they're on fire near the central-heating exhaust.

It takes four buckets to quench the fire.

Two Chinese youths move into another flat. They grow hash with hydroponics. Bio-fed hash. A ventilator goes off regularly at three in the morning – at first Dimitris and Zyna think it's a sausage maker – for the benefit of the hash.

The Pakistani couple move out because of the noise but the young Pakistani man still has a key and visits the house once a week, opening the accumulation of letters in the hall – casualties, traumas, mental hospital cases, junkies, psychopaths – reading them and leaving a litter of unopened letters on the hallstand.

One of the Chinese youths tries to sublet his smelly, claustrophobic room. Advertises for a roommate.

A black youth is a beanie comes, whose bumster jeans show boxers with a pattern of leprechauns. China youth rejects him and the black youth screams outside that he's been rejected because he's black.

The Chinese youth does have a Polish youth, whose black hair is so shaven his head looks like ash, staying with him for a while who's hit on the head at three in the morning on the North Circular Road, with a baseball bat.

There is an almost daily noonday concert of someone kicking the hall door and beating it with a chain. We take this in our stride. With Dimitris at work on a building site, Zyna wanders around in a pongee though Hannibal and Lecter are twittering louder than usual. It never occurs to us we should inquire into it. One January evening Dimitris had turned away a shaven-headed man with a prison tattoo on his neck 'Down for Life', who had come looking for me.

A junkie who looks like a mackerel head still attached to a bone body, a body of bones – an alleycat's delight – who's fleeing a drug gang in Coolock, and his girlfriend whose hair is a despairing flamingo, arrive and he immediately starts stealing bicycles, advertising them in *Buy and Sell*, amputating some of them, bits of bicycles all over the place.

Dimitris and Zyna play host to a youth just out of Mountjoy who showed up in Bermudas patterned with cheetahs and raj's palaces and raj's leopard-spot umbrellas, his legs golfball white, his entire belongings in a green Carroll's Irish Gifts paper bag, and their flat sounds like a fanatical rookery. They leave their door open at night and noise penetrates your room. They suddenly decide to play Panonski top volume, so you wake in fright as if being strafed by a helicopter attack. Feels as if a Balkan War is going on.

A woman is attacked on the street and her terriers – anklebiters – hanged.

I leave this savage Golgotha of microwaves that sparkle like a rocket about to take off, when turned on, or toasters that kamikaze after two slices of rye bread, of Dickensian hot-plates – one of the pair having given up the ghost – for another part of the city.

Shortly after I leave an old man who looks as if he's going to disintegrate or blow away like Traveller's Joy in autumn, comes to live in the house.

'I have come here to die.'

A black youth, drug trafficker, moves briefly into my room. He was born and bred in Galway but his parents are from the West Indies. Guards come looking for him and he disappears. The junkie comes down and robs money and his playstation from the next occupant of my room, a youth who looks like a frazzled snowdrop.

The postman had placed a book of Jean Leon Gérome reproductions for me in the junkie's arms one morning and I was lucky to have got it, that he didn't advertise it in *Buy and Sell*. I was lucky to be able to put the colour copy I'd made from it in my new room, Christ entering Jerusalem on a donkey followed by its milk-white foal, greeted by Mary Magdalen dressed as a dancing girl – an almeh – as a woman of Cairo.

The junkie frequently comes down and asks Dimitris if he has his bucket.

The junkies multiply like garbage rodents. The new junkie couple immediately sell the house hoover. He wears a hat all the time. The junkie who was already there hammers a hole in his door so he can shout abuse at the new junkie opposite who does the same thing with his door.

'I'll fucking break your jaw. I'll fucking break your throat.'

'Fucking handicaps. Fucking spastics.'

The junkie girl who was already there, nine months pregnant, has a knife fight with the new junkie's girlfriend, who in leggings has a plucked chicken look, cheeks enflamed – like a rare steak, and the old man downstairs drops dead.

Hannibal bites Lecter on the neck and Lecter drops dead. Then Hannibal dies.

Dimitris decides to put on his silver suit, white shirt, turn himself in at the Croatian Embassy with Zyna in her turquoise dress with matreshka dolls and Russian spring flowers on it, and ask for papers to return to Croatia.

Mosher and Peggy's Leg give them a Good Luck card which shows three children going up in a balloon basket.

'Sorry you're leaving.
You'll be missed.
It was nice knowing you.
I hope you return someday.
Have a nice flight.'

One of the main access points to the Royal Canal as it journeys from the Shannon to the Irish Sea, is in my mother's village in County Westmeath.

She wrote to me once about how she returned and visited the Church of the Nativity and knelt and prayed that if she had done anything wrong, that if she had made mistakes she should be forgiven.

The only people who offer you a meal in Dublin are a Croatian couple. This is before they leave Ireland. They wanted to make Scampi Buzara but there were only mussels available so it is Mussel Buzara.

Collecting date shells from the sea is forbidden in Croatia – they're not as old as the sixteen-hundred-year-old olive tree on Veli Brijun in the Brijuni Islands – but some are hundreds of years old and as soon as he gets home he hopes to get a tweezers, a hammer and sub-aqua outfit and dive for them.

When they go the city is lesser, lonelier without them, their stories of concentration camps and massacres and sudden, epic flights.

When they leave a golden thread is lost in the city – they've taken an Aladdin's lamp with them – something that on being messaged gives back images, stories, legends.

You follow the story as the raven flies into the teeth of the wind. Croatia bus and Dublin City buses have the same jazzy pattern navy and tango orange. They get their upholstery from the same company.

There are deer, goats, ducks in the fox-coloured hills and there's an exodus of foxes from the mountains to the lowlands – sign of a bad winter to come.

'We miss rashers, Leo Burdock's quarter pounder, fireplaces,' Zyna announces outside Isadora Duncan's villa, an annexe of a lamb's-wool yellow Austrian Empire hotel with marine-blue lettering, a tall palm tree Isadora Duncan loved beside the villa.

'We come from the Beverly Hills of Croatia,' Dimitris had told me in Dublin. 'Untouched during the war.'

'Isadora Duncan was killed here,' Dimitris proudly claims, who was handcuffed immediately on his arrival in Croatia and put in Rijeka jail for three months, later in the year getting a further two weeks for having magic mushrooms sent to him from Amsterdam.

'If you know everyone in prison it's not so bad.'

'Isadora Duncan wasn't killed here,' I contradict him. 'She was killed in Nice.'

No use contradicting a Croatian fact. Isadora's scarf became entangled in the wheels of an automobile here, in this town with its lungomare; its belle époque hotels all shades of yellow – Easter primrose, buttercup-yellow, old gold, rose-yellow, lemon-yellow, Naples-yellow; its Mediterranean-Gothic villas of Frankenstein hue; its youths like mahogany lizards, one of whom said to me: 'There was a were and refugees came here during the were,' its outbreaks of urban wood – chestnut, laurel, gingko trees, sequoias, holm oak, Japanese camellia, bougainvillea, baby banana trees, Japanese banana trees in which the soundtrack of *Elvira Madigan* is piped – Vivaldi's *Violin Concerto*, Mozart's *Piano Concerto No 21*; its German and Austrian tourists in Tyrolese hats, Alpine hot pants, white loin-stockings, with quarterstaffs; its historical list of visitors – Isadora, Chekhov, Puccini, Mahler, Coco Chanel (who was interrogated by the Free French Purge Committee for her Nazi connections but, unlike Arletty who was forbidden to act, was acquitted for lack of evidence).

'Before the war I was in the Young Communist Pioneers. Love your country.

Tito was a Croatian but he hated Croatians.'

'All the celebrities came to his funeral in Llubjana,' Dimitris breaks in. He's wearing a striped T-shirt – blue, white, orange, white, green, white, aquamarine, white.

'He loved being photographed with celebrities,' Zyna adds, 'Elizabeth Taylor, Gina Lollobrigida, Sophia Loren, Queen Elizabeth.'

'The Partisans stole my grandfather's bicycle during the war,' Dimitris complains.

'They threw the gold virgin who was by the sea, into the sea. She was put there by an aristocratic woman whose son was lost in a ship at sea. The Partisans replaced her with a maiden holding a gull. Bikers threw bottles at the gull during the war. The virgin was found and was put beside the church.'

There are button chrysanthemums under the Virgin now and a passing woman in a scarlet cardigan with a swallow at each shoulder flutters her fingers at the Virgin.

'The last witch in Europe was burned here,' Dimitris proudly announces, pointing to the beginning of a copse.

Never contradict a Croatian fact.

I knew there were executions of women accused of being witches in Switzerland and Prussia at the end of the eighteenth century and the beginning of the nineteenth.

Darkey Kelly who ran the Maiden Tower Brothel in Copper Alley, Dublin, which had a clientele of Hellfire Club young bloods, was partially hanged and publicly burned alive in Baggot Street, Dublin, January 1761. Believed to have been a witch for two and a half centuries, recently revealed as a serial killer who hid men's bodies in the vaults of her brothel, possibly the real reason for her terrible end.

'Never trust a cop or a hooker,' Dimitris would say.

Witch Hunt …

The template of prosecutions builds up, clerics who taught the classics. But I suspect, I know there's a lie. A misinterpretation of history.

'Tender grapes have a good smell …'

A priest who taught the Classics investigated the lonely Aughrim, the battlefield of a thirteen-year-old boy's body.

Flavio – gaunt eaten face like Saint Oliver Plunkett's, Russian camp pale rye haircut, ascetic glasses sitting on his face – plays his guitar on the lungomare on front of Isadora's villa. He was lost in the war for eight years. They declared him dead. His parents died. They took his house, cancelled his social security number. He doesn't exist. They looked at records going back to the nineteen thirties. He can't get a new number.

What is a person who doesn't exist supposed to do? He knew ten numbers on the accordion, including 'Lili Marlene' – 'The German version,' Dimitris is quick to say, 'Lale Andersen's version was played in Croatia all during the war.'

The Flavio got a guitar and he sits on front of Isadora's villa and plays all day, looking towards the shimmering round-the-year azure beloved of Hapsburg empresses and Russian tzars, sipping alcoholic beverages made from crushed walnuts or from honey and herbs.

Isadora Duncan had many homes. There is a statue of her behind Flavio. She dances nude among the shrubs grown from seeds brought back by sailors from their journeys. She dances to Flavio's tunes. But she knows that the last four tenants were recently evicted from another of her homes, the Carnegie Hall Artist Studios, including a woman poet in remission with cancer and a ninety-eight-year-old woman photographer, that this is the world we live in.

Sky and sea are a torrid thrush's egg blue at evening, a penumbra of orange on the sea and the mountains. You might expect the historical visitors to this place, Chekhov, Puccini, Mahler, Isadora Duncan, and even Coco Chanel if she wore black she looked best in, to come down from the mountains, a much-needed confederation.

When I first went to live in County Limerick after returning from England, in a dream, I came out of a pothole in the Warsaw Ghetto after the Rising. There were no survivors in my life. But there was a great menorah in the sky.

Zagreb is a hall of mirrors for me; it mirrors exactly past friends.

I walk through Zagreb from early morning to late evening, with its Popeye-the-Sailor blue trams, by the nineteenth-century paternalistic building, the Balkan stucco, the Stalin functional, the Stalin Gothic, the Stalin Titan, high rises with the words 'The Exploited' written at the bottom of them.

City of curd cheese and circuses. Tea towels with patterns of tiny owls or tiny houses with cloudlets above them and trees beside them cover shopping baskets. A man in a Stetson performs Gospel karaoke.

I frequently hear Freddie Mercury 'I Want to Break Free'.

Federico Benković, like Dimitris, exiled himself from Croatia, but returned and his *Sacrifice of Isaac* is tenebrist like the roasting chestnuts that are sold throughout the city – Isaac's head bent towards his adolescent genitals that are covered by a trail of gauze but we are reassured by edges in the painting that his pubes are growing. While his father points a dagger to kill him, Isaac is curious about his sexuality. His left nipple is bright as a girl's.

'Tender grapes have a good smell …'

'Zagreb was a bunker then,' Dimitris had told me. The Croatian army bombed Zagreb themselves. There were 10,000 skinheads in Zagreb during the war. Books by the white supremacist Matthew Broderick were popular.'

He was talking about another place when he told me: 'There was a man. He was the best neighbour. When the war came he lined thirty of his neighbours up in the corridor and shot them.'

As winter dark intensifies I am outside a barber shop with bay rum in the window in glass containers shaped like cannon guns or culverins – phallic – or in glass containers shaped like Prussian helmets.

On the wall inside a photograph of a nineteen-thirties barber in white coat standing beside a line of customers like people waiting to be executed.

In the shop window is a photograph of a modern counterpart, a youth in tank top, with teddyboy lip gloss, who doesn't look unlike Slavko's fifteen-year-old Albanian friend.

Zapamtite. Remember.

'I was in war. It's not a game of chess.'

They fought with hunting guns, bows and arrows, home-made grenades, potato mines, pineapple mines. They have grenades at home as souvenirs of the war.

Dimitris and I have been through the wars and once you've been through the wars you're marked, Toblerone and Turkish Delight may palliate, but you'll never forget.

Thornback Ray

'And what do you want the *Complete Grimm Fairytales* for, if you don't mind me asking?' the suburban librarian, in a low-cut sweater, with horizontal strawberry stripes, which left one arm bare, beside a Tucan twister plant (twisted and intertangled stem trunk), asked me as if she was thinking of calling the guards.

The Scottish fiddler and composer Niel Gow, who played for Prince Charlie at Dunkeld on his march south to Edinburgh, whose tune 'The Lass of Gowrie' Robbie Burns used as setting for 'Address to a Woodlark', when asked how he managed the long road home from Perth to Inver after a ball, said it wasn't the length of the road he minded but the breadth of it. He gave the distance as ten Scotch miles.

I don't know why I must retrace this lonely, lonely road out of Ireland, but I must. I must find this Icarus with a life sentence.

The stories the House Father (Social Worker) read to the boy were of journeys – 'The Wonderful Adventures of Nils Holsgerson' – a little boy turned into an elf and borne on a goose's back; 'The Snow Queen' – Gerda who journeyed, with nothing to protect her but The Lord's Prayer, to the palace of the Snow Queen to find her lost brother Kay; 'The Little Mermaid' – a mermaid who forfeited her mermaid's tail and her tongue and journeyed to land to find the Prince she'd fallen in love with; 'The Wild Swans' – Eliza carried by the eleven swans who'd been her brothers, who'd written with diamond pencils on slates of gold, praying to protect herself against the naked lamias who clawed open fresh graves, snatched up corpses and devoured the flesh as she was to collect the nettles she would weave to restore her brothers to permanently human form; 'Thumbelina' – snatched from the imminence of a marriage to mole by a swallow she'd revived from a state of death and borne to a land of blue and green grapes, lemons and oranges, myrtles and balsams; 'Thumbling' carried in a horse's ear, a cow's belly, a wolf's paunch; 'Aladdin' borne through the air by the Slave of the Lamp to a hamman made of jade, transparent alabaster, with pools of rose, carnelian and white coral, ornamentation of large emeralds, where he was massaged by young men of girl-beauty, washed with musk-scented rose water, given a sherbet of musk and snow and summer flower; 'Dracula' – the vampire Lucy Westenra trails children. Would the Social Worker have brought the boy to St Michan's and showed him the four mummified nuns and the mummified cat chasing a rat in the organ – one of the inspirations for Dracula?

To write with a diamond pencil on a slate of gold!

The Social Worker's writing was stilted, awkward, tilted to left, low self-esteem betrayed.

In prison one is cut off from history. One is cut off from source. Your existence becomes scatalogical. It becomes surcrease. One is robbed of imagination and if any signs of imagination remain – like tachiste (blotted colour) graffiti on the cell wall – you are driven into more extreme isolation. Like a mountain goat into a crevice.

The only option that remains is to end your existence with a garment ligature.

But the image, the reflection of the child remains to the end, Christopher (Christ-bearer) – Reprobus – carrying the child across the river, a mermaid, holding up her mirror, looking on.

When Christopher planted his staff by the side of the river after bearing the child, flowers and dates sprung from it.

When he was being tried in Edinburgh January 1978 the Social Worker remembered posies of goat' true and lad's love (old man, southern-wood) – dull yellow flowers that don't come in cool summers – were placed in court once to protect against jail fever from prisoners.

Ashes of lad's love mixed with salad oil for baldness or beard regeneration. Its kindred flower mugwort planted beside roads by Roman soldiers – to put in their sandals on long marches. Perhaps that's why mugwort still grows by waysides.

Near Glenochil Prison mugwort grows by the ruins of the Anto-nine Wall, ordered. by Roman Emperor Antonius Pius.

In Victorian times Artemesia abrotanum was symbolic of love between a man and a boy.

Because of love of a boy a life sentence in Glenochil, Clackman-nanshire – the smallest county – a male long-term prison.

Saint Begnet of Dalkey, who'd been betrothed to the son of the King of Norway, had made her way to Clackmannanshire from Cumberland and founded a chapel.

An angel had given her a bracelet in Ireland marked with the sign of the cross, as a symbol of her vocation, and by the twelfth century accusers and accused were asked to swear their testimony on the bracelet:

You've got to hold on to the dream no matter what. If you don't have the dream you have nothing. They don't understand. We lived in a dream for centuries; I killed to keep the dream.

Glenochil – a veto on your instincts, on your existence, on memory, the river in you.

The Cookstown and the Dargle Rivers met in Enniskerry, County Wicklow, where the boy scouts go. The head bottle washer of the scouts live nearby. The boy scouts would put black shoe polish on a tenderfoot's balls as initiation.

It was mostly Irishmen, their lodging separated from Scottish workers, who built the Caledonian (Edinburgh, Glasgow, Carlisle) and North British (Edinburgh-Berwick) lines. The Forbes family of Callendar House, where the marriage agreement between Mary Stuart and the French Dauphin was signed, did not wish to look on a canal so in 1822, the Union Canal, longest canal tunnel in Scotland, was cut through by Irishmen, many of whom were killed by rocks.

New publications section of Edinburgh Annual Register for 1813 cites 'Glenochil', a descriptive poem by James Kennedy in two volumes.

Robbie Burns, who was knighted in Clackmannanshire with the two-handed sword of Robert Bruce, wrote his last poem about the River Devon near Glenochil Prison.

'Crystal Devon, winding Devon ...'

The River Devon rises behind Ben Cleuch, highest peak in the Ochil Hills, which you can see from the North side of Glenochil Prison, and joins the River Forth (five and a quarter miles away as crow flies) but takes over thirty miles.

The Ochil Hills as you can see them from the north side of Glenochil Prison have slashed deep ravines, steep gorges, sides swooping without foothills directly to flats as a consequence of the Ochil fault that plunges thousands of feet below the silted-up flood plain.

Mary Queen of Scots attended a wedding in 1563 in Castle Campbell on those southern-facing slopes and John Knox administered the sacrament of the Lord's Supper on the grassy slopes between castle and cliff.

'Pity me, Kinsmen, for the sake of Jesus Christ, who pitied all the world,' Mary Stuart's young husband Lord Henry Darnley cried as he was strangled outside Edinburgh, naked but for a nightgown.

Murderers with life sentences were on the third floor of A Block in Glenochil, sexual offenders on first floor of A Block. Sexual offenders' windows were blacked out. They were known as The Beasts. Bags of excrement and urine were thrown at them from B Block and C Block.

There was a tropical fish tank on life-sentence floor – leopard catfish, suckermouth catfish, salt and pepper catfish, pineapple pleco, orange-cheeked pleco, panda corydoras, black dwarf corydoras.

Lifers have nothing to prove. They just want to get on with life sentence.

The Prison Chef had previously been employed in the Dorchester – a 4-Star hotel.

There were three metal gates between educational building and the blocks to deter metal objects. You could learn hairdressing in the educational building. You could learn engineering, tap and dye, iron casting.

The adjoining coalboard offices were turned into junior offender cells.

One-hour visits were allowed.

There was a man in Glenochil who made fudge in the microwave from Bounty Bars, sweetened condensed milk, Nesquik Milkshakes.

Prison workers, trained in mouth-to-mouth resucitation, regularly found bodies.

Glenochil has the seventh highest suicide rate in Scotland.

'If they get pipes out they can hang themselves from them. Can electrocute themselves with wires.'

They could hang themselves with electric wires, aluminium wires, aluminium piping, metal cages.

Beds were bolted to the floor but if they could get them up they could hang themselves from them.

They could hang themselves from low bar cells if they pulled their legs up.

There were searchlights in Glenochil prison yard.

'Being gay was a terrible thing in Glenochil. No maturation. No development.'

'I swear by the Blessed Trinitie
I have no wife, no children, I,
Nor dwelling at home in merrie Scotland.'

The boy had the probation genitals of a nine-year-old, like a butterfly orchid.

Scorched by bath water in an Edinburgh hotel, opposite Waverley Station, his body, found on the Feast of Giovanni Bernadone, Saint Francis of Assisi, looked like a common spotted orchid white as the top of the Himalayas.

'It was just horseplay,' the Social Worker, who was found with sixty-nine tablets, told the police.

The Queen had asked a huntsman to kill Snow White and bring

back her lung and liver. Snow White's coffin had been made of transparent glass.

In Mount Jerome Cemetery, where the boy was buried in Saint Luke's summer, the thinnest fox lives.

It was believed in Ireland a child would die if raven's eggs, pale blue to pale green, were stolen. A raven lives in the Scots pine in the cemetery – nest a cup of dried grass, moss, lined with rabbit fur.

Buzzards pass from Wales, hovering over the cemetery, maiowing like a cat, mobbed by jackdaws who try to settle on their tail.

A family of sparrowhawks live in an abandoned crow's nest in poplars by the River Poddle in the cemetery.

Saint Charles of Mount Argus lived nearby, who cried during passages of the Sacred Passion and who'd cured a boy of blindness, the boy later becoming a Carmelite priest.

A Russian youth stokes the ashes in the crematorium now.

Did the funeral party – mother, mother's mother, mother's sister, stand among the poppies with white beards by the Grand Canal and watch an otter crunch an eel?

Reflections in Snow White's transparent coffin. Inner Dublin streets.

The Roma Café in Dorset Street that sold thornback ray – humpy ray you ate, off the bone.

A lemon, lighted-up fish with scarlet arrow, flickering on and off, on his back, pointing the way into the chipper.

A boy in scarlet jersey suddenly veering vertically across the road in disregard of the traffic, onto the opposite pavement, like a cardinal bird let loose in these parts.

Sean McDermott Street in snow, like L.S. Lowry's paintings of Salford, ensembles of tiny figures adrift, muted, made a joke of against the Titan blocks of flats.

A woman wheeling a pram full of king-size Twix bars.

Skin-heads with baby-bottom haircuts.

Youths in hipster jeans with Mick Jagger haircuts.

Youths in diamond-pattern jerseys with Eric Burdon and the Animals haircuts – plastic, side-swept quiffs.

Pot belly stove in an orphanage and a picture of Mary on the wall, who looks as if she's had a ghetto nervous breakdown, pointing to her heart,

To find your way home with white pebbles that glitter in the moonlight like coins. A duck individually ferried Hansel and Gretel across an expanse of water on their final journey home.

The deepest and loneliest part of the wood where a white bird brings you to a house whose walls are made of gingerbread, roof of cake, windows pure sugar.

The boy's family – mother, grandmother, mother's partner – considered they were having a sexual relationship. Those in authority tried to separate them. What's sexual at seven, eight, nine? Sleeping naked together, touching, fondling?

When someone has had a sexual relationship at six they may later in life seek sexual relations with six-year-olds, A man in their part of Dublin – where, when a medical school was turned into a national school, barefoot boys played hurling with human bones and skulls, where Matt Talbot ate dry bread, drank cocoa without milk or sugar, slept on a plank with a wooden plank for a pillow – joined the British Foreign Services and sought child prostitutes in Asian cities. When someone has had a sexual experience at six they may later in life like looking at photographs of nude six-year-olds – red smartie penis on small ball of genitals.

A birch tree grows outside St Giles Cathedral, ragwort and fleabane by steps leading to the castle.

The Royal British Hotel opposite Waverley Station – Scottish baronial turret, Dutch windows, dormer windows.

Disney shop underneath it now.

There were mobile statuettes on the top ledge, moving theatricals. The statuette of Pinocchio fell apart on the ledge and became dangerous and had to be removed. Bits of it could have fallen on customers.

We have a cowslip-blonde Alice in Wonderland with the Cheshire cat, the Mad Hatter in what looks like a mock football supporter's hat, samovar beside him with Russian flowers on it, the March Hare with cake; the Little Mermaid with nineteen-forties roll top, lilac bra, tail that looks like single green legging, Flounder the Fish; Dumbo the Flying Elephant with his one friend, Timothy the Mouse, in brimmed hat; the house of Gipetto, Pinocchio's maker; six brooms from Fantasia; Pluto, Minnie Mouse in yellow-and-strawberry polka-dot dress with cup sleeves, using a vintage camera; a smaller Minnie Mouse in red-and-white polka-dot with matching ribbons; Mickey Mouse in very short shorts with two white eyes on them that could be taken to have a sexual meaning.

When you wake or are woken at night you try to hold something the way the Little Mermaid held the drowning prince, brought him to shore, saved his life. You try to bring something to shore. You try to salvage something.

Your train journey to Edinburgh was theirs, past sea-houses, Saint Cuthbert Island where the saint lived as a hermit, inner Farne Island where Saint Aidan from Galway would spend Lent, where Saint Cuthbert lived in solitude and died. The Farne Islands are a sanctuary for birds and seals now.

On the main door of Durham Cathedral where Saint Cuthbert is buried is the Santuary Knocker – tongue of a demon with holes as eyes, flews on his face, dog's ears, aureole of sunrays.

Knock it if you murdered someone and you get thirty-seven days sanctuary within the Cathedral and a possible chance to flee the country.

'O spare my life! O spare my life!

O spare my life!' said he;

If ever I live to be a young man,

I'll do a good chare for thee.'

I feel I am the one running away from Ireland with this boy – running away from ignorance, medievalism, chasing some truth.

There's no truth in the land the man and the boy are fleeing.

It's a land of lies.

Victorian béguinage architecture – tower rooms, dormer windows, turrets, iron crosses with circles in the centre; titanium and ichorous statues of the Sacred Heart; spring heather and hebe; larch trees, yew trees.

Hebe, Goddess of youth, Ganymeda her other name, but it was Ganymede who was chosen here.

I ask where the Child Care Centre was.

'Was that where all the abuse was?'

An avenue of lime trees (*crann teile*) with trunks covered in ivy as if to hide some shame.

National Park lodge-house type apartments with bird tables outside.

The name of the house has been changed to Hawthorn.

Embassy of Islamic Republic of Iran nearby, St Andrew's Presbyterian Church, St Philip and St James Church of Ireland with its pines, firs, arbutus.

'Are you treasure hunting?'

There was no Aladdin's cave like that boy.

Face like a wren's egg in a lost property department, white, delicately speckled reddish.

The red of the fox against the yellow of the winter dunes; his hair was like that. Eyes like the dog violets sprinkled in the emerald-green dune moss.

In his smile was a journey on a goose's back, in the clutch of eleven swans, in the clutch of the Slave of the Lamp, on a swallow's back, with his feet on the swallow's outspread wings bound by a girdle to one of the swallow's strangest feathers.

Beechwood Road, Ranelagh, Leenane No 18 – Cambridge-blue door.

Yukon No 15 – glass door. Nanvilla No 13 – Staffordshire terriers in transome. 12 – pale, too pale terracotta. Roundel mosaic print lawn pathway. Chinese puzzle hedges. Claret-and-yellow glass windows at back of house.

Beechwood Road – pampas grass, sumac trees, lots of schoolboys in blue the same colour as the door of No 18. The House Father, the Social Worker lived No 12.

1977. The lonely year. The year of leaving. The year 364 heads of Old Testament Kings, decapitated on the facade of Notre Dame in Paris during the Revolution, were found when they were digging the foundations of a bank in Paris.

The year of trying. Of running away. Of wanting to be lover to a boy-child.

Close by the Hiberno-Romanesque Church of the Holy Name in Albany Road where the Social Worker faithfully attended Mass.

Did the Social Worker have zealot's features, some hurt, some deprivation from childhood challenging you? Was he a culchie? He had one previous conviction though it's not stated what for. Did he and the boy sleep in the same bed in flight? Did the boy wear blue pajamas with a pattern of soccer balls?

Did the Social Worker sing lullabys to the boy — 'The October winds lament around the castle of Drumore … Clan Eoan' s wild banshee' — as a nurse used sing *Marlborough s'en va-t-en guerre* (Marlborough has left for the war), composed the night after the Battle of Malplaquet 1709, to Marie Antoinette's children as a lullaby?

Did the Social Worker have dark algal pubic hair like the hair the little mermaid's sisters cut off so they could get a knife from the sea-witch that when stuck in the prince's heart would bring warm blood that would restore the Little Mermaid's fish-tail?

In the Ranelagh Take Away as it begins to snow there's a small boy with a flamingo band running over top of head and down back of it, tall, older brother in habit-brown tracksuit.

Love is a stranger in Dublin. Love belongs to another decade.

Truth is another time, another country.

'I'll get you a cup of tea, one slice of toast, one sausage in Bewleys,' I once heard a small pawky boy with pink freckles like sweetpea say to an unwhetted Croppy from Wicklow or Wexford on Grafton Street.

A decade when Tattens — Large Coffee (Kathleen Toomey), ashy bouvant., geranium lipstick, with Mount Merrion accent, from a part of Wicklow with stubborn homesteads, mad cows, rams with Methusaleh beards, used jog, carnation in lapel, with a large coffee and a Mary cake — biscuit base, chocolate filling, almond icing, mint embossments – to her pet customers in Bewleys Grafton Street, so eager was she to deliver them.

Tattens started her workday with a prayer in Clarendon Street Church.

Used holiday with young waitresses in Gran Canaria, Lanzarote, Tenerife, dress up in her evenings there in white cotton blouses, flower-printed collarless blouses, white flower-printed cotton dresses, white straw hats, blue leather shoes, bead necklaces and earrings, and chat in red hotel lobbies to Guanches boys – descendants of the blond-haired people who'd originally lived on the Canaries.

Mayerling was a big hit in Dublin then, about Rudolf, Archduke and Crown Prince of Austria, who committed joint suicide in a hunting lodge in Mayerling, fifteen miles south-west of Vienna, with his seventeen-year-old cousin, the baroness Maria Vetsera, on the morning of 30 January 1889.

So was *Elvira Madigan* about the twenty-one year-old German-born circus acrobat, her step father John Madigan the circus owner, who was shot by thirty-four year old Swedish Cavalry Lieutenant Sixten Sparre in the forest of Neorreskov on the Danish island of Taasinge, with his service revolver, after they'd made love for the last time in Renoir haze on 1 July 1889, he then ending his own life in similar manner.

'Danced she on a tightrope lightly
Glad as the skylark in the sky.'

Cleopatra was frequently recalled to Dublin in which Elizabeth Taylor is borne into Rome on a Sphinx and in which she commits suicide with an auraeus – cobra – bite, following Richard Burton's suicide as Antony in the same month, August 30 BC.

You frequently found yourself looking at a poster for *Cleopatra* with Rex Harrison as Caesar gazing at enthroned Cleopatra like a lascivious vicar.

Grallatorial boys – long legged like the football teams of herons who stalk the water edge – would wander the dunes of North Bull Island then seeking sexual pick ups. Milkshake-coloured bodies. They used soother cream — antiseptic lotion — or white cream for scabies for suntan lotion. They'd exchange sex for Carroll's cigarettes or Lemons Sweets. Brylcreem. Toothpaste. Toothbrushes.

They assessed clients the way the foxes who live in the dunes assessed intruders.

The fox knows how to offset himself against the harebells because it is photogenic.

A fox had got into Dublin Zoo looking for small creatures and a polar bear ate him.

To fool the rabbits on Bull Island. They used put down nets for the hares on Bull Island, have greyhounds chase them. They would put down nets in the dunes the way trinkermen would put down trink-nets — fixed nets in the Thames in Elizabethan times. They'd block off a rabbit holes, pin nets down, send ferrets in after rabbits.

Winter evenings when the sunset looked like a sleeping fox and the dunes were fox-coloured.

The man and the boy ran away September: month of the fox, month of the harebell.

'She had an alcoholic husband who died. The Social Worker wished to foster the child. The authorities tried to separate them. Decided to run away with the boy. He was affiliated to some Christian Brothers.

It was a culture, an otherness with the Christian Brothers. They had a hard life. The Church treated them badly.

It was an attraction to innocence, by taking innocence you destroyed it, possessed it.

He had a burden of otherness. He ran away with the boy and murdered him in this otherness.

It's also about control. You can control. End the life of a nine-year-old boy.'

Gerald Griffen from Pallaskenry, County Limerick — mutton-chop locks, widow's peak, girl's brows and mouth — given to high talk, turned his back on his literary success at the age of thirty-five in 1838, entered the Christian Brothers after burning his manuscripts in the manner of Gogol, devoted the remaining two years of his life to teaching poor boys at North Monastery, Cork.

His play *Gissippus*, which had failed to find acceptance during his lifetime, produced at Drury Lane 1842, part of London just north of the Strand where signs saying 'Beware of Sods!' were abundant.

When the boy was in the care of the Social Worker the rent boys of the Inner City would gather in all-night cafes and speak a Polari, a cant of their own – a scatological cant.

One of them was found floating in a stone-washed denim suit in the Liffey between Burgh Quay and Georges Quay.

In one of those cafes there was an advertisement for Wrangler Jeans on the wall: 'Let Wrangler lead you from the straight and narrow.'

The ragazzinos from Sean McDermott Street, some of whom speak Polish now, fish in the Liffey now for eel, mullet, crabs, using a rasher from Lidl as bait, which they fling in the Liffey when finished.

It was a tug-of-war between mother who loved the boy and wanted him back, to whom he'd run home his last Christmas from the suburban orphanage, and the House Father, Father, Social Worker, who wanted to adopt the boy, be father to son. The mother, the family, insisted there was a sexual element to the relationship.

In his flight from Ireland the Social Worker brought a photograph album, photograph folder, loose photographs.

Were they Kodak photographs with white borders?

Naked, shorn of clothes, the boy was as pale, as pastel as the cuckoo flower – curvaceous too, a little Cupid, a little Amor.

In V-notch briefs white as rabbit in a fox's mouth and after the summer his skin beige as the hares that sat on the golf course.

Naked, his penis and genitals were like the beige and nervous catkin of the hazel tree.

Naked, his body and penis were as white as the eggs of the wood pigeon, whose nest is a thin untidy platform of sticks in a tree or shrubs, his buttocks thin as the pigeon's untidy platform nest of sticks in a tree or shrubs.

Genitals like the ravishing bee-orchid with its pale purple Doge's hat above the bee-lip.

Nudity like the last snowdrops.

'... make my grave both large and deep,
And my coffin of green birch.'

'O younge Hugh of Lincoln! Slain also With cursed Jewes!'

Little Saint Hugh of Lincoln, aged nine, disappeared 31 July 1255, scourged, crowned with thorns, finally crucifed, body found floating on water, hands and feet pierced with wounds, forehead lacerated. Buried near tomb of Robert Grosseteste, philosopher bishop of Lincoln.

Copin, a Jew, admitted murder under torture. He and eighteen other Jews hanged. Chaucer refers to Little Saint Hugh in *The Prioress's Tale*.

The golden-haired subject of many screen paintings, twelve-year-old William of Norwich, a skinner's apprentice who'd frequented the homes of Norwich's Jews, was found on Household Heath, Thorpe Wood, north-east of Norman Norwich, which still exists, in March 1144. A one-eyed servant woman claimed she'd caught sight of the boy fastened to a post as she was bringing hot water to her Jewish master. Thorn points were found in the head, lacerations in the hands, feet, sides. Accusation that he was shaved, gagged, crucified, were made against the Jews,

On 6 February 1190 Norwich Jews who didn't manage to escape to Norwich Castle were slaughtered and those who escaped to the castle committed mass suicide.

Jews were expelled from England in 1290, many repatriated in Spain.

1492, after the Edict of Expulsion by Ferdinand and Isabella, the Jews of Segovia spent their last three days in the city in the Jewish cemetery, fasting and lamenting over their dead.

'If his boyhood is reason enough for rejecting his holiness, we remind them of those boys Pancras ... and Celsius.'

Pancras, a Phrygian orphan, was beheaded in Rome at the age of fourteen, his body covered in balsam by a Christian woman and buried in the Catacombs. Mentioned in *Martyrology of Bede*. Relics sent to Oswiu, King of Northumbria, by Pope Vitalian around 664.

Celsus, a nine-year-old boy from Gaul, painted by Titian and Camillo Procaccini, was taken in a ship after Nero ordered him to be drowned, thrown overboard, but a storm arose, frightening the sailors, and he was pulled back on board. He was later beheaded in Milan.

Tarsicius carrying the Eucharist to confessors in prison, and to Presbyters in other churches, was attacked by a pagan mob on the Appian Way with stones and clubs. Buried in the Cemetery of Callistus. He is the patron of altar boys.

The boy was altar boy age.

Skeletons found in the Tower of London 1674 are thought to be those of twelve-year-old Edward IV, a boy-child in ermine in an illumination in Lambeth Palace Library, and his younger brother, Richard, duke of York, probably murdered on Richard III's instructions in the Tower, August 1483.

Gerda travelled to the palace of the Snow Queen with nothing to protect her but the Lord's Prayer ... In the fourteenth-century the bell-maker of Breslau wanted to create his masterpiece for the Church of St Mary Magdalen – the Sinner's Bell. In anger when his young boy apprentice interfered with the plug for the metals he stabbed him through the heart. For centuries, up to the end of the Second World War, when the part of the church where the bell was situated was destroyed by explosion and fire, the Sinner's Bell tolled for The Lord's Prayer.

In medieval Christianity the Feast of the Holy Innocents was the last day of the Feast of Fools, last day young boy bishops had authority. In medieval England boy-children were whipped naked in bed that morning, a custom that survived into the seventeenth-century.

Perhaps the goose woman of Kassel had told the Brothers Grimm a version of *The Pied Piper of Hamelin*.

The Lueneberg Manuscript 1440–1450 states that in the year 1284 one hundred and thirty children of Hamelin were seduced by a piper in divers colours and murdered near the Koppen (Old German for hills).

More likely it refers to the Children's Crusade – twelve-year-old Stephen of Cloyes who led 30,000 children to the Mediterranean at Marseille, expecting it to part. Nicholas, a ten-year-old shepherd from Cologne, who led 20,000 children across the Alps, a loyal contingent of them to Genoa, where they were refused transport across the Mediterranean.

None of the children of the Children's Crusade ever reached Palestine. Many were taken as slaves to Tunisia. Many died in shipwrecks.

Norwich Jews who didn't manage to escape to Norwich Castle were murdered.

A man's house is burned in Dundalk. A man's house burned in Newtown Mountkennedy, County Wicklow. A man's house is burned in Cavan and his cat burned alive.

A man is knifed in Donegal.

To go the way of the fox, another way, not their way. Tell the crows how beautiful they are and ask them to sing. Can a crow sing a folk-song? Can a crow tell a story?

'And I'll pike out his boony blue een,

Wi' ae lock o his gowden hair,

We'll theek aur nest

When it grows bare.'

Why does a fox cross the road? To get to the other side. I was never very good at jokes.

A boy said to his Mammy, 'Mammy, there's hair growing on my willy!'

'That's to keep you warm when you're swimming,' she said.

I was good at telling fairy stories. The fox will be out in an hour or two. To stroke you was like stroking the fox at evening.

There was an Irish Traveller in Glenochil called Maugham.

The Social Worker hung himself after ten years in the prison.

If you lose the narrative – the way the Little Mermaid lost her tongue and power of speech, the witch cutting her tongue out and then giving her a draught from a cauldron cleansed with snakes, sounding like a crocodile, one of the ingredients of which was her own black blood – you might as well be dead.

Hansel reassures Gretel that God won't forsake them, finding their way home with the help of a duck.

Finding your way home.

Being in prison you miss the shelduck with beak red as war paint, black belly stripe from breast to vent, who nests in rabbit holes.

Being in prison is like going into the depths of a cave in Lascaux or Trois Frères to scratch a painting of a horse in bone or stone, hennaeing the hide in, making it into a fire, painting a human face – the soul of the horse. In prison you are scratching a picture of a boy-child in bone or stone on a prison wall, making his freckles and his hair into a fire.

Being in prison you miss the spring sunlight on the red-brick Georgian houses of Buckingham Street, an inner city grimalkin-granny giving a wallop to a child in a red polka-dot St Vincent de Paul dress who refuses to be reproved.

Never again to see the early flowering cherry tree in first blossom beside St Patrick's Cathedral.

Never again to see Wicklow saturated in primroses.

'Hello Mr Magpie, how do you do?

How is your wife and your children too?'

'I buried my own daughter,' a woman with crocheted white cap like a golf ball on her head tells me outside the ichorous – dried blood – Lourdes Church. 'She died of neurophagia. Aged three. They moved me out to Finglas after that. I stayed there three weeks. Then I came back to Sean McDermott Street.'

She remembers the boy's mother.

Harem scarum fringe, tuberous lips, baby girl with corkscrew fringe in her arms, blubber in her mouth.

'She lived in the tenements. There was Spanish blood somewhere.'

The smell of the tenement corridors, like a cardigan soaked in urine. And you were likely to encounter rats. Rats go for you. You get bitten on mouth. On ear. Rats and their legends were Royal. Like the Georges under whose reign the houses were built. The railings were taken away 1932. Intercoms came late seventies.

'Rents were five shillings or seven and six. But they didn' t have it.'

The moorhen has a roof I remember.

'Bailiffs parked cars at Garda Stations. They used catapults on them.

They burned floorboards to keep warm.'

And then she spiels about namesakes of the boy's mother but probably not her people.

'The grandmother lived on top of Mary's Mansions. The children used collect cabbage leaves, potato skins, hard bread on the balconies and bring them to her pigs. She had pigs in a shed in Hutton's Place behind the Bus Garage. They sold sea eels and salmon heads, Manx kippers and thornback ray on a stall in Parnell Street. Manx kippers were saltier. You had to soak the Manx kippers to get the dye out. They were up at five to buy the fish on Little Mary Street.

Maibe got a flat in Liberty House. It went on fire. She had the windows locked because of the children. But the children weren't there. They tried to break her windows with a pick and couldn't. Even if they did the oxygen would have caused the flames to get worse. The place would have gone up in flames. She died, she did. It was the smoke.'

'You're a fucking nuisance,' a woman with hair arrangement like a boxing glove, in black and white, *langue-de-chat* harem leggings, addresses her small child in its pram as she passes.

My informant diverges to namesakes of the boy's alcoholic father, probably not his people at all.

'They lived in Brigid's Mansions. Sheriff Street. Long knocked down. The eighties. The men were dockers. The women had stalls. Sold Dublin Bay prawns. Sold anything they could get their hands on. They'd sell yourself if you stood still. They were funny people. Had a sense of humour. You had to have. Some of them got mickey money.' (Compensation for alleged abuse in Industrial schools.)

'There were Robin Hoods in those days. Commandos from the Second World War. They used catapults, ball-bearings, made traps with fishing tackle and clothes pegs for the Christian Brothers and Guards who came to take the boys away.'

As slave ships sailed up rivers in West Africa in the eighteenth-century so young strawberry-faced guards went into Sean McDermott Street, picked up boys, sent them to Industrial Schools, where they sought the warmth of the chapels as the pied wagtails sought the warmth of the Christmas lights on the plane trees on O'Connell Street.

'There was one fellow who was in Artane for stealing. He was kicked to death. The mother went to the Brother and asked for money for the burial. The Brother said he could be buried in Artane. The mother got a hire purchase coffin. He was buried in a pauper's grave in Glasnevin.

There was a man who was in an Industrial School and he married a woman who was in an Industrial School. They had six children. Both walked down steps into the Liffey.'

A stocky mother passes holding hand of a daughter with Down Syndrome, the girl's hair clubbed at the back by black embroidery. She has earplugs. Her stride is springy.

'I better hurry on. I'll miss me Lotto.

Go and see the priest.'

The priest's cardigan is ash grey but his eyes are the green of tartan bartered in the Atlantic towns of Mayo, a little of Stuart Hunting green.

'There were millers down the docks. The dockers had slashhooks, machetes to pull cargo. Containers came in 1965. The dockers were laid off.

When the 1970s came some of the youths got high-power rifles, some hunting rifles. Some joined the Republican Movement. Some turned to crime. Some to heroin. Heroin came in the seventies.'

A bedlam of boys from Mary Mansions attack me with snowballs.

'Leave him alone,' says one with hair the colour of crusts of Brennans sliced bread.

'Stop that,' comes the megaton accent of a woman sitting like a Budda on front of a basket of plastic lustre flowers and some tchotchkes at one of the windows of Mary Mansions.

'I'm writing a poem about my dog now,' a woman wearing glasses with blue frames, with a lantern chin, a Dutch cut, carrying a handbag with a pattern of mallards in all kinds of states – swimming, standing, flying, spreading their wings, tells me outside Lourdes Church. 'My last poem was about my friend who died in an orphanage in Wicklow.

Saturday night was writing night in the orphanage.

We ran away once and went to Bray.

We'd heard there was a call girl in Bray aged forty-two.

We had fish and chips in Papa Lino's. We rode the golden gallopers. We had chips in the Capri before we went back.

She used always come into my dormitory from her dormitory at night and whisper in my ear.

One night she didn't come in and I went looking for her and she was dead.'

'Pillycock, pillycock, sate on a hill

If he's not gone – he sits there still.'

'I can smell the shite off you!' says a boy who looks like a balloon blown up, with a Dublin accent coming out of a balloon, to a boy with hair the autobiography of a fox, outside Lourdes Church.

Two seconds to go and it's on me knickers.'

In almost uniform tracksuits the youths look like an army. People at war. Sean McDermott Street is an ordnance survey, a map of war.

Thornback ray ...

Vietnamese, Chinese, Thai, takeaway fronts say now. There's been a Dog Found notice in marker on one of their windows for years.

Boys dart out of sidestreets near the takeaways at dusk like nightjars, the bicycles making a sound like the Irish name for nightjars – *Tuine Lín* (flax spinning wheel). Nightjars were the *Púca* bird.

'Sweet Pucke, You do their worke, and they shall haue good lucke.'

A dwarf in a T-shirt with a reclining girl in stocking boots, drawstring bikini, passes with a poodle on a leash.

A man in a wheelchair wearing a stars baseball hat with stripes under the peak.

A man in a blue-grey T-shirt with a grey snarling hare's head on it, the hare' s mouth outlined in scarlet, emerges from a sex shop.

'Is that a hare?' someone asked me, 'Only a pubic hare,' I told him.'

'In this part of Dublin cousins go with cousins and brothers with brothers. I went with thirteen-year-olds. Is there anything wrong with that?

At ten they played with one another. The older ones brought the younger ones home, played Kings and Queens. Ten-year-olds were the Queens. Had to strip. Lie on the bed.

It was common for fathers to have sex with sons. Sometimes the fathers would have sex with sons when they were six.

A man tried to have sex with Waldi Handiside when he was

fourteen and when he wouldn't go along with him the man hung him from a rowan tree the Corporation put there. Passersby cut him down and saved his life.

There was a gang rape then by a gang on Sean McDermott Street. Umbrella up vagina. Nipples cut off. The girl died.'

Sean McDermott Street boys in prison got prison tattoos – biro and ink, thread around ballpoint – of swifts on their wrists. No legs, tiny feet.

The swifts returned beginning of May – clung to the Georgian walls with their tiny feet. When on the wing approach their nests, bang on them with a wing, without landing.

Began return journey to Africa beginning of August.

And the man finishes:

'I started putting on my mother's stretch satin mini-panties when I was twelve. At fourteen staying with my aunt on Tonlagee Road she caught me in her mini-length silk slip. She was very understanding. She was a Ladybird.'

I look in the mirror to see where she lives now.

'Mirror, Mirror, on the wall, who in this land is the fairest of all?'

She disappeared into a broken mirror.

'People change their names by deed poll,' the priest tells me, 'Marry again.'

A woman passes us in fuchsine mules and dressing-gown, with a tan from California Sun in Ballybough.

Edenmore. Donnycarney Church. Darndale. Oscar Traynor Road. Tonlagee Road. St Margaret's Estate. Popintree.

You move to these parts but it's a way of seeing things, a way of being alive.

You miss the insomniac swifts.

You miss the funerals with the piper with the pony-tail, sleeper in ear, black covert coat, crocus-gold kilt who leads the corteges with a coronoch of pipes, women pulling on cigarettes as they await the arrival of the hearse and coffin.

You miss the streets Matt Talbot walked on with chain on waist, chain on one arm, on the other arm a cord, a chain below the kneecap of one leg.

You miss the thornback ray.

'A woman stayed on ten years after they tried to move her out. Fourth-floor Foley Street.

(Legion of Mary cleaned it up in the 1920s.)

Eight flights of steps up. With only the light of the Fiesta Club, Talbot Street. or the security lights of Ruttles Clothes factory.

She got tinnitus from the noise of the nightclub.

A neighbour brought an electric stove. She had no water. Youths would have rocket fuel (cider) parties at night. They came with jack hammers on the roof and threw things down.

The pubs were closed. The neighbours gone. She died of a broken heart.'

The legends of Wicklow where the little boy spent his last months, having run away from the suburban city orphanage, back to his mother: the raven spilt Saint Kevin of Glendalough's milk when he was a boy and Saint Kevin cursed them and they couldn't land on his Feast Day 3 June or get food — they had to rely on their caches of food under rocks or crevices; an otter brought Saint Kevin salmon for his nascent community; a black bird hatched her blue-green, finely brown speckled egg on his outstretched hand as he prayed.

A three-year-old boy had been scalded to death in a hot bath in this orphanage in 1947.

A panavision family of foxes lived nearby.

Early March the blanket of snowdrops on the lawn became like a hankerchief someone had cried into,

The sharp rush — *an luachair bhiorach* — large, pointed tips, grew on the nearby coast, where there was a strip of clandestine beach, white as monastic voyager's sails.

There was a brother and sister in the area in their sixties who were having sex with one another. He wore a tea-caddy on his head.

The orphanage was burned down purposely end of the eighties. A Vocational School, an old building, was also burned down, same way, about 1995.

A Church of Ireland rector was stabbed to death during a night robbery.

When a man has had a sexual relationship with a very young boy, sometimes the boy has been accidentally killed – strangled usually, asphyxiated.

The yellow-and-black striped caterpillar becomes a tortoise-shell butterfly with hindwings that have dark margins towards the body containing bright blue crescents. Towards late summer – when the Social Worker from the suburban city orphanage collected the boy in the Wicklow orphanage, after the boy had run away to him a few times – the tortoiseshell butterfly basks as long as possible on meadow trails or-sea trails, clasping the earth with its wings, to absorb as much heat as possible to prolong its life.

'Why are people attracted to pre-pubescent boys?' you ask.

'It's the moment,' is the answer, 'Some of those who are say their fathers were like that before them. It runs in the family.

It's also about control. You can control.'

Control.

End the life of a nine-year-old boy.

Some of those Brothers were like Pygmalion, a King of Cyprus, father of Adonis, who carved an ivory statue and then fell in love with his creation, the Goddess Venus bringing the statue to life, or like Gipetto the Woodcarver who carved Pinocchio from a piece of pine. The altar boys, the nine-year-olds with cathecism bodies, were statues or wood carvings brought to life.

'Some priests, Brothers were too shy for thirteen and fourteen-year-olds. Thirteen and fourteen was too old.'

Did the Social Worker give a birthday card to the boy on his ninth birthday, his final birthday, with Arthur Rackham's Old Woman who lived under a Hill on it – an old lady in a witch's hat, skirt patterned-with pink flowers and apple-green foliage, zebra-striped cat beside her?

The hour of the Witch ...

Hansel and Gretel managed to shove the cannibalistic witch into the oven in which she'd planned to roast them.

In a London guesthouse did they sleep together under a bed-spread patterned with a soccer player and the same soccer player on the purple pillows?

The frog managed to get into the Royal bed.

But the princess threw the frog against the wall in disgust and he became a prince.

To the grey Georgian brick of Edinburgh against the red Georgian brick of Dublin.

The dying little Match Girl lit a match on New Year's Eve, which made the wall she was lying against transparent, and saw a Christmas tree with thousands of candles on it, the ultimate candles becoming stars that took her to death.

A bath in an Edinburgh Hotel.

The bath in Marlborough House on Washerwoman's Lane was sexual folklore.

Erections at nine the way Pinocchio's nose grows larger when he's lying, pubes at ten.

To trace the vines of the everlasting pea in the dunes until you come to the pink flower like a small boy's genitals.

Snowdrops become ghosts in the grass in March.

It wasn' t murder, it was a mixture of horseplay as he said, and sexual play.

The Social Worker took an overdose after the boy drowned. 'It is just a pity it didn't work for me,' he told the police.

I like solitary and rare birds like the yellow wagtail who peruses the seaside streams.

We live in a world where the Slave Aesop's goose has been murdered ... There are no more golden eggs, no more dreams, no more running away.

The Spindle Tree

'Wally, wally wallflower, a growen up so high. We are all children and we shall all die.'

Some people carry their precious possessions in a safe.

In my life there was no safe.

Today I looked at family photographs, photographs of my mother, my father, myself. Childhood. Hometown streets. All decimated by a year and two months in a caravan in West Limerick. People, myself, streets, looked as if they'd been through a terrible war.

They had.

Wishing time to pass more quickly, you're wishing your life closer to death, he used say as he took liquorice pellets for his throat.

Alexis of Rome, he told us, left his wife on their wedding night and went on a long pilgrimage.

Joan of Arc heard the voice of St Margaret of Antioch, the shepherdess daughter of a pagan priest, who was swallowed by a dragon, which then burst asunder.

There was a boy in the class whose cream face had blue shadows running through it – victim of a bone disease. His mother, in scarf, with Native American mouth, would chaperone him around town. 'Bapty, come in for your two blue duck eggs,' his mother would shout at him as he wandered off by himself on Jubilee Street. She was always going in and coming out of the Presbyterian Hall behind the

Presbyterian church where the Drama Society rehearsed. Maybe she cleaned there.

Sophocles, Mr Ronazeyne told us, died aged ninety-three, from eating a bunch of grapes sent to him by the actor Callippides.

One of the almost indecipherable photographs showed Mr and Mrs Ronazeyne with a class gathering, and I could see that Mrs Ronazeyne was wearing one of her patterned scarves.

I remember those patterns: baby deer in green polka-dot dickie bows on black, rabbits in jaunty tams, with handbags, crouching frogs and spread-eagled frogs, ladybirds on ebony black.

She had a mare's face with colours of a plum leaf in autumn, hazel eyes of a poodle who'd been crying, and people would stare at her as she walked with Mr Ronazeyne as if she was General Tom Thumb – the Barnum-Circus dwarf who on his marriage to another dwarf, was received with his wife by Abraham Lincoln – because it was known she'd tried to cut her throat.

'I had a little husband
 No bigger than my thumb.'

They'd take a long walk on winter evenings, carrying a baked potato in tinfoil, passing people in coats so great they were unmappable.

Their house at the beginning of Hearse Road had a nursery-blue-door with Georgian transom, amber leaf pattern in transom, glass onion dome above and above that again oblong stone with relief work, sky-blue outline to the windows.

Outside the door was a stone puppy in stone basket, stone frog beside a stone mushroom.

The yellow irises that flourished in May by O'Kelly's Castle from which a Royalist Commander had once flung himself during a siege into the moat and so to safety in Spain, are a symbol of childhood for me, of adolescence, of the River Suck, of East Galway – *an Tachadh Réidh, an Achréidh* – the smooth field.

The house and the garden once belonged to the Woods, a draper family whose shop on Main Street had been stoned so many times during the War of Independence and the Civil War, that it partly inspired a letter of condemnation of attacks on Protestant businesses from the bishops in Maynooth in October 1922.

One of the Woods still lived in town, a hump-backed man who

rode a motorbike with a covered side-seat. He'd ride that motorbike to an Orange parade in a town just south of the border, a town of nearly all platinum-haired Protestants.

He befriended a youth from Custume Barracks Athlone with eyes the blue of twin hyacinths and would sit in the local hotel – the Claridges of the West – with him.

I remember the silhouette of Mrs Ronazeyne as she watered her snakeroot – brilliant azure, purple, mauve, white – in July.

The Woods' garden.

I'll begin with the trees: the Dombeya (the pink snowball tree) – a late autumn and winter tree; the early flowering cherry, the Mount Fuji cherry tree of spring – 'Next week the blossom will be gone,' she'd say, the mock orange, the California lilac tree with its deepest blue flowers, the orchid tree, the Chinese wisteria, the bitter-sweet, the Royal Star magnolia, the Spanish dagger (yucca tree) of summer and the crepe myrtle, again in autumn the red-heart hibiscus and the primrose jasmine.

The flowers of spring: Bells of Holland – white and Eton blue and mauve, the beetroot primulas, the yellow inula, the globe daisies that lined the walls, the lilies of the valley, the white pearl hyacinths, the Blue Angel alkanet, the New Zealand satin flowers, the blue Kingfisher daisies, the elephant-eared saxifrage.

The flowers of summer: English marigold, Venus navelwort, bear's breeches, white Apache plume, garden loosestrife, golden splendour lilies, African Queen lilies, butterballs, heavenly blue convolvulus, light-blue English lavender, harebell poppies, pheasant's eye, hedgehog broom, Kent Beauty origanum.

The flowers of late summer: tomato-red crocosmia, dark mullein, goat's rue, borage, evening primrose, belladonna lilies, Dolly Varden geraniums, Blue Danube ageratum (floss flower), blue butterfly delphiniums, onion, blue pea, shamrock pea.

The flowers of very late summer: phlox, St Catherine's Lace, the rainflower, Jacob's Ladder, the Cape Gooseberry (Chinese lanterns) that flourished only after a very hot summer when the boys of St Brendan's Terrace walked like rangatiras – Maori chiefs – by Shallow Horseman's, if wearing anything, wearing their mother's long-legged knickers.

In winter there were the white flowers of the Poison Arrow (wintersweet).

One September she was seen carrying a red-hot poker and its leaves in a tote bag and the following August there were four red-hot pokers – torch lilies – in her garden.

But it was the spindle tree – the *crann feorais* – that I went to look at in all its variations.

Late autumn the leaves of the spindle tree are withered and dying, interlocked with the distraught madwoman's hair of the tuzzy muzzy (Old Man's Beard).

The spindle tree in winter, like a naked boy, or like the hyssop on which they gave vinegar to Christ.

Childless, terrified, she always had a lighted candle in her window at Christmas when nuns sent a memo requesting tinsel paper after Christmas.

You could see the candle through the arms, the entanglements of the spindle tree.

February when leaves came to a branch or two, tuzzy muzzy still entwined with the tree, a branch or two in leaf like the arms of a menorah.

Often the first leaves of the spindle tree would be killed by a cold spell.

Tiny little upright scarlet buds of the spindle tree when fog of the tuzzy muzzy has retreated.

Colours of autumn in Lent – rose-bronze, copper-green, purplish-green – when black sole was sold by Somme veterans in Market Square, door mats (big ones) for the well off, slips (little ones) for the poor.

Spindle tree in August ochre.

Always autumnal, in autumn the spindle tree was dragon-flame red.

When you see bluebells in plantations you know they've been growing for hundreds and hundreds of years. Likewise the spindle tree in old plantations and hedgerows.

Once used for spindles and pegs. Small elegant fruiting bud becomes a berry the finches and tits and house sparrows are fond of.

There was a curmudgeon sweetshop proprietor with a ponytail

who wore a Home Front pinafore patterned with coloured cows on white whose father had fought in the First World War. 'He fought on the Jellylines,' people would say and call him Jellylines.

Children would go into her shop with the family name in azure outlined in cream above, and ask for a penny worth of Jellylines, whereupon they'd be chased with a lemony bristled broom that Anna Lee, who was inspired to leave her husband in Toad Lane in Manchester in 1774 and go to the United States where she got Shaker followers who, like her, believed original sin was sexual intercourse, might have used.

I had the temerity to go into the sweetshop one day, put up to it by a boy with two snag teeth the colour of yellow chewing-gum who always quoting Hotspur – 'You'll laugh your head off at this week's red circle story,' and request a penny worth of Jennylines, whereupon I was chased with that Shaker elder broom.

I took refuge by the spindle tree's rose-tinted, copper-green leaves, smaller curlicue rose leaves, tiny oriental fires.

Like Joan of Arc Mrs Ronazyne heard voices.

Shortly before her death she went around town collecting for a priest in Sweden who was starving for want of financial support. It was her one public act.

The Greek hero Meleager's mother Althea ended his life by burning the log that was contiguous with his life.

An early flowering cherry tree can flower fitfully. Hers was in flower that December. She drowned herself in the Suck by Murrays' Bridge. Her funeral was on Christmas Eve.

She'd made a rich cherry cake and the story was the cake was served at her own wake.

'A chapter was over,' people said.

'Where are you going?' her husband asked as she left in a scarf patterned with stuffed foxes and rocking chairs.

'I don't want to be found,' she said.

People came and took white flowers of the wintersweet as people had taken the earth from around the grave of Mary MacKillop in Sydney after her death.

Knowledge is to be made aware of grief and suffering.

When someone lives their life with great integrity, with great devotion to beauty, they cast a shadow after death.

Her spindle tree was a vademecum for me – it shed stars on your life like those of a chandelier.

On one of my returns to the town I saw the For Sale sign beside the spindle tree.

Having seen the oleander trees and the sweetgum trees and the sumach trees and the fig trees and the mulberry trees of the Southern States I went back to the town searching for the spindle tree and I found that subsequent owners of the house had not only cut it down but also destroyed the garden. Only the mock orange remained and a border of Kent Beauty origanum gone wild.

There were abacuses in a window and lots of space for cars and lots of cars.

'Bapty, come in for your two blue duck eggs.'

I feel like Mr Ronazyne now as he hesitated before the blackboard, trying to remember some fact, an anecdote.

Autumn nighttime in Mrs Ronazyne's garden when the English marigolds went to sleep, the evening primrose (sundrop) – spotted red – opened up, the red-hot pokers – torch lilies – kept nightwatch, the light-blue English lavender was a still bright moat border.

Now a motorway bypasses the town. People go to Galway and Limerick to shop. The status, the remembrance of small towns has changed.

But I remember it.

I remember the spindle tree.

The Metlar

'Limerick is proper bad,' says a mulatto youth from Wolverhampton, glittering stud in right ear, baseball hat with Fair Isle pattern and NY on front that his girlfriend bought for him in Birmingham, who has just returned in the apple-green Dublin coach from visiting a child of his in a child-care centre there.

The Shannon has changed pattern. In winter high tide there are catastrophic floods at the Metlar – Metal Bridge. Swimming, swimming horses, conversations are impossible.

Saint Ciarán of Clonmacnoise once consigned a chasuble to the Shannon waters and it arrived safely to his friend Saint Seanán at Scattery Island on the mouth of the Shannon. I want to send a chasuble back to Limerick. I want to put on Hans Christian Andersen's Galoshes of Fortune and visit the Metal Bridge.

Maybe I'd meet Pasco – autumn oak and rufous glib (fringe), a puzzled foxcub, in his T-shirt with a monkey putting a record on a record player, there.

He pointed a steel-pellet gun at me once at the Metal Bridge.

'You can use bullets in it too.'

'Where did you get it?'

'In China.'

'When were you in China?'

'Two weeks ago.'

'Where in China?'

'I don' remember. Name a few names.'

'Shanghai.'

'It wasn't there.'

But Pasco was killed by a car on Sarsfield Bridge. I was already living in Dublin where looking for something lost was like walking through the vast First World War cemeteries in Flanders or the north of France. In Limerick the River Shannon was sovereign. In Dublin there is no test.

We all have our sacred sites.

Aborigines.

Native Americans.

Ourselves.

Alders were the first colonizers after the Ice Age. In spring the catkins of seed alder trees – alder woody shrubs – make an intense radiance on the ground by the Metal Bridge. The juvenile leaves are different from the adult trees, they are candelabras on the ground later in the year. Mangy foxes come and drink tidal water.

There was a witch hazel tree – tree of healing in the Spanish Civil War – in yellow bloom one December Saturday when there was a sunken car, upside down, wheels showing, in the Shannon.

'There are more rabbits here than people in Moyross,' a youth whose head looked as if there was a kipper flattened on top and one on each side, in track suit but unusually not plimsolls, but shoes of true white with kind of silver or diamante decoration on them. There are five thousand people in Moyross.'

I'd just seen a sponge on a stick outside a house in Moyross with R.I.P. in marker on it.

The windows of the house were blanked out with blue Christmas paper with gold Christmas trees and a galaxy print.

'Instead of going to Mr Binman's on the Ballysimon Road where they'd have to pay to dump, they dump here. They burn plastic, keep copper, then go away and sell it.

There were always faction fights in Limerick coming towards Christmas. Into jail for a few weeks. Get your hair cut.

Dell pulled out this year.

The Kileely boys have their own scramblers (Kawasaki) and the Island Field boys have theirs.'

Island Field was on the other side of the Metal Bridge.

'You wouldn't know what you'd find if you walk on Island Field. A gun. A bag of drugs.

They built railings at the Metal Bridge to prevent people crossing but the people knocked them down so they could swim at Corbally Bank.'

'My friend jumped off the Metal Bridge in 1978,' a man in a mud-green baseball camp, with as many medals on his chest as those of the queen on a gala night – John Paul white as a snowshoe hare, black and amber Byzantine medal, Cancer Charity badge – 'I am aware', Byzantine cross fretted with a miraculous medal, told me the same day.

With his walking stick and stance he looked like one of the veterans you see outside the Royal Chelsea Hospital.

'Left a suicide note. Worked on Shannon Industrial Estate with De Beers South African diamonds. Westing Company House was there too. They made components for rockets. Limerick was a different place then.

Went to England to get rich after my friend committed suicide. They didn't give me a knife or a fork.

Bob Giles was the candyman in Croydon. Used to go up the Pearly Way, past the aerodrome, with copper tanks and old fridges on his cart, a concrete barrel for balance. He had a Welsh cob called Amy.'

In Dublin Kileely is a street song in my mind.

'For I take in old iron, take in old bones and rags.

And all other different kinds of stuff,

And I put them in separate bags.

I've travelled this country o'er, and I'm known to everyone.'

The ragman used give toffee in exchange for goods and that's why he was known as the candyman.

Youths like ichneumons – insects who deposit their eggs on other insects' larva to feed their own larva – shepherded horses toward the Shannon under birch, fir, sycamore, laurel like the moss-overgrown oaks of Louisiana. Asarbacca still grew along the edges of the path. Vaparettos went by on the Shannon, canoes with outboard engines.

Later children rode up to Freda's Takeaway, beside The Great Wall Chinese Takeaway, on Shetland ponies, two on each, a small child holding a big child from behind.

'The chips will take a minute. The chicken will take eleven minutes,' declared the chipper girl with the lightest of eyebrows, baby baby gloss, caviar-coloured nail varnish, beside an advertisement for Circus Gerbola.

At Limerick bus station before I got the bus back to Tralee where I lived, with the simple rye bread of friendship I bought at Limerick market every Saturday morning, a youth with copper hair a farmyard fowl retrospective began staggering around the station concourse, reciting aloud:

'They hide in the skies
They tell the lies
They're the ones who played with little boys
God is a she
Not a he
I may be sad
I may be mad
But on the final day I'll be glad.'

Traveller youths in slinky leatherette jackets, skinny jeans, pillows in hand, stop me on the way to the Metal Bridge on a January Saturday, a day of war rainbows, of discarded teddybears in scarlet party dickie bows and discarded net American football tank tops.

Accent soft as Pecker Dunne singing 'Portlaoise Jail', a Croagh Patrick Reek Sunday or Garland Sunday mist.

'I'm Square. I'll give it to you for a tenner.' Square has peacock-blue lining to his hood.

Another with azure T-shirt showing, says 'Happy Christmas,' as he thrusts a pillow at me.

One with three half-braids on outer hood — silver, gold, blue — tells a story in attempting to sell a voluptuous pillow.

'Gizmo Glavey is a schizophrenic. His friends tied a rope to a horse and threw the rope over the prison wall. Gizmo caught the rope before the screws could catch him. The fellows on the outside goaded on the horse. Gizmo landed on a mattress. Gizmo escaped. He'd put three old women in the boot of his car and drove them around for three days. Something was wrong in the brain.'

A Traveller girl in white satin figleaf hot pants, mini-bridal veil on her head fastened by diamante, torture spikes on her high heels, will tell your fortune at the Metal Bridge by looking at her mobile phone and playing John Hogan 'An Old Cottage Waiting in the Country' on it.

'I bought a shocking orange top, a shocking, shocking pink top, and a holy statue of Our Lord.'

Another in Cinnecitta vermilion vies with her.

'I bought a lemon-and-peach top, mini hot pants, and a candlestick holder with Padre Pio on it.'

It was all about segueing, the Metal Bridge, one thing leading to another, making connections, just as youths climbed the grids in the summer, bit by bit, ultimately to jump off.

Life deals out a savage lot to some people but the name of the guards is always on Bella's lips with some accompanying anecdote that puts her and her companions in story-telling mood.

'The guard — the mudguard — is a big man. The Hulk. A girl would like him. A woman wouldn't like him ...'

Against a harvest, a wheat of yellowish-white willow catkins Bella wears coin earrings with surround hoop earrings, has a toothless mouth, alligator smile, raven hair, wears a country-mourning black cardigan.

Three of her children were burned to death nineteen years ago in a caravan at a halting site in Briton Ferry, Swansea Bay.

There was a guard of honour of Traveller girls in black at Carroll's Funeral Home, Listowel, County Kerry.

But Paz, her son, kissed all the girls in Field Drive with his long mouth, colour of pickled beetroot.

Steel, her own husband, got eighteen years in England.

'Sure that was life.'

He was in Brixton Prison. Couldn't go to the tuck shop. Had to ask for everything he wanted out of a catalogue.

Danzum has eyes blue as a voyage through the Straits of Messina. Is featured in the photograph of Hyde Road football team in The Yellow Road takeaway, Boherbuoy.

In Stab City, in a T-shirt that says 'I'm Grumpy. Don't make me any worse', he stabs the Metal Bridge with my calligraphy pen, frightening a copper mustard and green black frog.

'Pakistani, Pakistani.

Does your mother have a fanny?

Is it smelly?

Fucking hell.'

The cannon guns of Limerick always looked as if they were going to issue smoke.

Limerick street boys are frequent urinators. They urinate alongside the cannon guns in the evenings, buttocks turned to you in a manifest way.

Gaius Marius, Roman general and intriguer, nearly seventy, practised weapon drill and riding, oiling himself and playing ball on Campus Martius – the Field of Mars – among the youths throwing the javelin and fencing who, oiled and dusted, jumped into the winter Tiber.

'Smoking is bad for you,' I say to one of the Kileely boys who haunt the Metal Bridge as the wren does, some collecting frog spawn, toads, newts.

Prawn-coloured Cupid's bow lips, deep furrow above lips, coconut-milk skin, puppy brows, stud in left ear, facial expression of a field mouse who has just said Amen, he's wearing a scarlet baseball hat with white cartoon-button eyes on it, peach nose, black outline of mouth.

'It makes you grow.'

The stories I hear here are like the shadows on the wall in Plato's Cave but a Plato's Cave full of Nobelaner beer bottles, Kopparberg Swedish cider bottles, Everyday Essentials spaghetti in tomato sauce tins.

'My son is laid out,' says a man with hair a half-forgotten sienna on top, stubs of grey at ears, stubbly face, Roman patrician's nose and mouth, in polo shirt scarlet colour of Carroll's cigarette packet.

His son was drowned a few days before while swimming at the Metal Bridge drunk on Polish beer.

'Sorry about your son.'

'It's alright.'

Pan Sausage John – this name is tattooed on his left hand – surveys a periwinkle growing among Samson tobacco papers with lion's head and a teddybear in a surcoat, with glasses with missing left wing.

'They've been like that for months. But it's alright. I'm getting two new pairs in two weeks.

The Doughans are going to Germany. Slugger is very bad. A Traveller. He'll be left in a wheelchair.'

A Traveller boy who lives in a winnebago – motor home – in South Hill, calls you 'Bud' and requests cigarettes, swims naked at the Metal Bridge, blessing himself before swimming – slight, workhouse buttocks, pubes a fugitive chestnut, that of a squirrel running up a tree.

'You're a Hogan. But not a Hogan like me,' says Runoo, who has shaven sides, dyed actor's black, urban art olive-yellow, semi-permanent dye on his fuzzy crest.

'In a hotel in Killarney on ee's I found a pink handbag. Handbag in one hand, mobile phone in the other, trying to find out who owned the handbag. Guards raided. I was in the cell 6 pm to 2 am. A guard shaved off the hair on top of my head.

The young guard who shaved off the crest on top of his head had a face like Jacob's Mikado biscuit, pink coconut with red jam ridge in it.

'I'm going to put Jah Cure, "Behind these Prison Walls" on my phone. He was in prison. For raping Jamaica. But he says he didn't do it. And Gregory Isaacs. His teeth fell out from cocaine. He's dead now.'

'My sister was going out with someone they didn't like,' says Nacho, a youth with hair like a cider tsunami in a white T-shirt with woman's open red lipstick lips with bullet in mouth. 'They turned against me. They broke into my mother's house in Moyross where I was living. Took silicon off the windows. Burned the house. I moved to my mother's boyfriend's house in Ballynanty.'

By a dwarf fir tree that has a bee orchid growing under it I witness Nacho's pit bulldog Einstein, not out for four weeks, jump at the mouth of a thoroughbred tethered with sex-shop vermilion reins and headstall as if she was a girl who gave massages, the thoroughbred taking Einstein into the air, Nacho picking up a stick to get Einstein down.

Nacho's Rottweiler babe has recently had pups and a rat bit one of the pups and he died of hepa-virus.

I begin a group-contributing story with the boys by the Metal Bridge on a day when some are carrying long rosaries with large wooden beads – kind of wood children's toys are made of – they got from monks in mackerel gowns, rain anoraks, who were reciting the rosary outside the New Vic Card Club on Hartstonge Street. A woman in spike high heels, pencil jeans, with hurricane blow-dry blonde hair, had joined the monks.

It's from Winky I hear the first part of this story, this history; black half-moon eyebrows, dark eyes, ammunition above his Royal blue anorak. There is fear, trauma in this boy. He has been torched.

('I was charged with dangerous driving on a push-bike and possessing a butter knife.')

Cooler takes up the narrative; baby-blonde hair, Madonna-blue horizontal stripes of two different shades in his Bermudas, vanilla-darkening to his legs, white ankle socks – as he tells his part of the story he contemplates his own sad state.

('I was scammed. But I only got six months.')

'He has the smallest mickey I ever saw.' That's what the other boys at Saint Brendan's National School on Rosbrien Road used say about Teddyboy Creedy. His family had goats in the front garden on Rosbrien Terrace.

There was a man with a toad's head in uniform, with steel bicycle clips always on his trousers, who worked for the Harbour Master, in bonded whiskey depot.

He threw peanuts at Teddyboy Creedy's mickey.

The Dundons, Clohessys, Callopys, Ingles, Houlihans, Bardinis, Bennets went to that school.

They were given a glass of milk and a currant bun every day there.

Stringer Agnew's mother gave him a Cadbury's Club bar each morning and he used give it to Teddyboy Creedy for protection.

He was always wild people said of him and that he stuck a flick knife in the neck of the headmaster at Saint Brendan's at the age of twelve – a man with hair enbrosse and loop glasses – but that must have been just a wrangle because Teddyboy Creedy swam every summer evening undeterred at Corbally Baths, crossing the Metal Bridge to get there.

He'd stand in the middle of the Metal Bridge for both sides of the Shannon to see, in pansy black drape jacket with fur-lined collar, tea-black waistcoat, mortuary-black shirt with white buttons, charcoal Slim Jim tie, high-waist drain-pipe trousers, white socks, white beetle-crushers with black soles, melon lips, with Boston haircut-greased back roach, square cut at the back.

The man who worked for the Harbour Master used to give him presents of Wella for Men, non-greasy hairdressing.

He'd pick yellow irises to bring home to his mother in Rosbrien. Daffodils he called them.

'If there's a breeze on the Shannon you catch nothing,' the fishermen on Island Field would say to him.

'The small eels I throw away. You peel off the black skin of the big ones and there's a lovely white flesh inside.

You can't eat a salmon that's just spawned. It would make you sick. Throw it back. Belly all tissue.'

He was banned from Donkey Ford's chipper but a girl with sardine-blue eyeshadow would bring a chip butty out to him.

'Say hello and what's your name?' he'd ask the man who took an interest in him as he stood outside The Red Rose Café on Parnell Street, smoking the butt of a Carrell's cigarette, or 'How are you John?'

He'd tell them jokes.

'What did they say to the ham sandwich when he came into the bar?'

We don't serve food.

What do the monkeys get for their lunch?

Half an hour.'

For some reason he'd often sit at Limerick bus station nearby as if he was waiting for someone to arrive but no one was coming at all.

When his mother was pregnant with him and not well, the doctor would advise her to have a Craven A cigarette – ' Have a fag' – and this was ventured as an explanation for his state of being.

He'd cycle on Limerick's pavements and Neanie Bohan, who always attended the Pioneer Total Abstinence Annual Meeting at the Gresham Hotel, Dublin, who walked a flood of white poodles, would abuse him – 'I have a right to walk me dogs.'

Used cycle around Limerick with a smaller boy with face like a bread roll with a smile in it, on front of the bicycle, cigarette butt in his mouth, challenging other cyclists to a race.

There was a sixty-year-old barber in Wickham Street – hot towel shaves – and Teddyboy Creedy called him 'My bud'. Teddyboy Creedy always tried to be last in in the evenings to have his hair cut so he'd still be there when the door was shut.

With his creamy-white hair and protuberant body the barber looked a bit like a cauliflower.

You could leaf through *Adonis* in the barber shop – male physique artistry, Body Beautiful – which promoted beefcake, Man-ifique – more slender males, Formosus – men with spray-on sweat in G-strings, feet resting on javelins, *Boxing Illustrated*.

There were pictures alongside the mirror of a topless girl holding up a clothes iron with the caption Much Too Hot, blonde Handy Morgan grasping a cushion for all she is worth in Godiva Rides Again, a lady with right breast bare pouring a drink for herself on a drinks cabinet, Saucy Susan – black dress dipping to show melon breasts as she admires herself in a hand mirror, and the Three Stooges on orange-red background – Moe in a red-striped shirt cutting Curly Joe's hair with garden shears while Larry is about to cut Curly Joe's nails with a machete.

The barber used bring Teddyboy Creedy to the picture house – the Savoy or the Grand Central or the Carlton or the Tivoli or the Thomond, but only when there was a *Carry On* film showing.

Carry On Camping – a horned goat butting Joan Sims' backside in pale-blue panties.

Carry On Cruising – Dilys Laye in micro-red bikini fleeing a sea captain in white, white cap too.

Killer Keaney – who killed someone in the ring – taught Teddyboy Creedy to box at Shauney's Boxing Club on North William Street.

Teddyboy Creedy in toy-vermilion tank top, shorts, leather boxing boots, luxuriant arms but with the pallor of the detritus of cat's milk.

His grandfather Padas in Moyross, blind, still drove. People in other cars stopped out of respect for him.

Teddyboy Creedy claimed he lost his virginity at twelve, and indeed, white bobby socks pulled up over his trousers, he'd be seen like twelve-year-old incubus wrapped around a girl who wore a dress with a pattern of choc ices and lollipops.

'I feak the béors. They're waiting like pups for it,' Teddyboy Creedy announced.

Teddyboy Creedy was no longer a Teddyboy, a cosh boy, a spiv, when he was sent to jail. He wore a wine T-shirt, swastika medallion, leather jacket like Sid Vicious.

A youth with hair like diced carrot presented him with a Royal William red rose on its stem, picked from a garden beside a kiosk with Our Lady of Fatima in it so Our Lady of Fatima looked as if she was ringing the guards.

'You're going to go to jail.'

In Limerick Jail bullies took tobacco from other prisoners and Teddyboy Creedy would make them give it back. 'I put them back in their shells.'

In Portlaoise Jail cell windows were broken in hot summers. They weren't taken swimming but sky-diving at Baldonnell and maybe up in the sky in a plane Teddyboy Creedy remembered himself swimming at Corbally Bank in briefs the orange of March coltsfoot flower and at evening, when everybody was gone, in nothing at all in Corbally Baths – slight, raspberry jam on white, sliced-bread buttocks, and maybe he remembered too, like one of the men chained to a chair in Plato's Cave, watching the shadows on the cave wall from the fire behind them, the light of the sun on the alder woody shrubs at the Metal Bridge and on the pyramidal orchids and the Marsh Helleborine and later in the year on the pale blue scabious that intermingled with meadow foxtail and wheaten Timothy grass like medieval livery.

Teddyboy Creedy saw *Carry on Cleo* with his barber friend: two Ancient Britons travel to the glamour of classical Rome and Egypt but return to their cave where the people they shared adventures with – Mark Antony, Caesar, Cleopatra – would have been shadows on the cave wall, just as they would have been shadows on Teddyboy Creedy's cell wall in Portlaoise.

Returning to the cave from the Metal Bridge – an urban grenade of abuse was thrown at me in Kileely one July Saturday after a news story broke.

The story of Teddyboy Creedy was broken off with the shadows of Cleopatra, Mark Antony, Caesar.

Waterboatmen the Kileely boys called the crane flys – Daddy-long-legs – who waded on the Shannon surface at this time of year.

But there were no boys.

Just lines that had been with me since childhood when my mother had brought a volume of Shakespeare with starved-crow-coloured covers back from a bookshop adjacent to the Halfpenny Bridge in Dublin.

'... on Nile's mud
Lay me stark naked, and let the water-flies
Blow me into abhorring!
... islands were as plates dropped from his pocket ...
Now no more
The juice of Egypt's grape shall moist this lip ...'

Swimming at Metal Bridge was like swimming among sharks – the sharks were wrecked or torched cars pushed into the Shannon.

The Japanese knotweed flourished when I returned to the Metal Bridge in mid-September.

There was no one about.

I saw a bar-tailed godwit, red on breast after summer in Greenland, beside a clump of three-veined sandwort.

A robin meandered toward me.

In County Limerick if a robin was caught in a trap instead of a blackbird or a thrush, it was never killed. The robin after all had followed Mary on her flight into Egypt when she was out from brambles and dripping blood, and covered her trail with leaves.

The brambles by the Metal Bridge were full of blackberries.

When I first returned to Ireland from England I stayed with an old lady in Connemara who would send me blackberrying and then bake haemorrhaging blackberry pies.

I'd seen houses burned out in Moyross, Limerick, and after my flight into Egypt, that was what it was like in Dublin; migration from one room to another. One area to another.

Relocation they called it.

Past those sleeping out, past the sleeping bags.

'What did you do to my cousin, you poufter?' a girl in a T-shirt with a pink lion's head on it and in Ugg boots that emulate the maned legs of a cob horse had shouted at me on New Road, Kileely, on my way to the Metal Bridge.

The River Acheron was thought to go through Hades. Oracle of the dead on its bank. River of Woe it meant. The river in Hades.

The Shannon had become a River of Woe for me.

Swimming at the Metal Bridge had been like swimming in the Pactalus where King Midas got rid of his golden touch, renewing touch with Achelous, the River God, god of change.

But the Metal Bridge had become sinister.

Neptune had been River God before being promoted to Sea God.

Achelous was River God but so was Cephisus, the father of Narcissus who fell in love with his own image in the river and, unable to possess it, pined away in sorrow and became a narcissus.

Teddyboys run in the family, generation after generation.

Daffodils the Kileely boys called the yellow irises that grew by the Metal Bridge.

The Traveller girl who told fortunes by the Metal Bridge could bring up a photograph of John Hogan, the country and western singer, in scarlet jersey, hands clasped, on her mobile phone.

On my way back through Kileely a man who looked like a corgi wearing a panama hat, tattoo of a sizeable pistol on his left wrist, braces with a pattern of pale brown rectangles, with a copper Petit Brabancon dog, a kind of dog that used to be used in cages on coaches to warn trespassers or intruders off, shouted my name.

Nacho had moved from Ballynanty to a second floor flat on New Road, Kileely, and he called me from the window and invited me in.

His head shaven now but for a Cleopatra's asp of hair on top of his head.

'This is an aspic's trail, and these fig leaves

Have a slime upon them such as th' aspic leaves

Upon the caves of the Nile.'

His girlfriend Serina — hyssop-honey bouvant, dark brows — wore a T-shirt with a black-and-white tiger with her cub on it, both with candy tomato noses.

Two photographs in frames had come with them from Ballynanty.

One of Serina at the Debs Ball, Greenhills Hotel, Ennis Road, in a deeply décolleté dress with oriental lady's face on it with red lips, blue eyeshadow, pendants on forehead, ring finger on breast, canary-coloured ear pendants.

Another, of their teenage friend Miley who had recently died – vinegar and cider complexion, in a Fair Isle jersey with blue ducks sailing on upper blue band of a different shade on it.

Miley had been called after his father. He had a sister, two brothers.

'No farewell where necessary,' Serina said.

Perhaps the ducks on Miley's jersey were the teal you can see at this time of year at the Metal Bridge, Nacho said.

They offered me tea and I said I didn't drink tea but I had a slice of suicidal chocolate ganache cake wearing an overcoat of desiccated coconut.

'A celebration cake,' Serina called it.

'We're celebrating Miley,' I said. 'We're celebrating the Metal Bridge.'

The Kerry Crozier was found by an O'Sullivan of Tomies while he was fishing in the River Laune near Dunloe Castle, Killarney, in 1867, six years after Queen Victoria's visit to the locale. The staff covered with bronze plates silvered over, the crook, the lower end, the bands, divided into decorated panels and overlaid with gold. Bears a close resemblance to the eleventh-century Lismore Crozier. In all likelihood lost or hidden by Bishop Richard O'Connell when he was hiding in the vicinity from the Cromwellians.

In Kerry I was made to feel like Pope Formosus, his body dug up by the Synod of Cadaver, put on trial in a throne, a deacon alongside the corpse answering for him, his fingers of consecration cut off, just as the hands of Cicero, in whose time the youths still swam in winter in the Tiber at Campus Marius – the Field of Mars – after exercise, were cut off, Pope Formosus' body put in a grave, later thrown into the Tiber in the way the Romans of Cicero's time threw criminals executed at the Gemonian Stairs into the Tiber.

On Saint Martin's Day I managed to get the last bus from Tralee as a Jewish woman once told me she'd been on the last train out of Vienna as a child just before the war.

Saint Martin of Tours was betrayed by the honking of a flock of geese when he tried to hide among them, before being appointed bishop.

He got revenge by cooking one for dinner.

During his military service in Amiens, France, he'd given half his cloak to a beggar who turned out to be Christ.

The house martin, called after Saint Martin, never builds its feather-lined nest of 2500 separate tiny mud pellets where there is strife.

At Tralee bus station there was a man in a ten-gallon hat and open primrose western shirt, right upper arm of the shirt slashed, blood stains on it.

'That's Runer Furlong,' a woman in a two-tier coat of mail – flash lilac and silver links – wearing flash lilac earrings, with crimson hair, said to her banana blonde cowgirl companion with cotton cowboy handkerchief and in stirrup boots.

'Hatcheted his brother-in-law on the street over a drugs deal gone wrong. Jailed. Let out for his daughter's Holy Communion. She wore a tiara from Prize-Time at Casserly's Fun Fair.

Now he's out again. A funeral up at Saint Martin's Park.'

At the back of the Bus Éireann there was a very small woman in a crab jump suit who looked like the achondroplastic – short-limbed – dwarf jester Maria Barbola in Velásquez' painting *Maids of Honour*, who implicitly looks at Philip IV and Isabel, unstated but for a reflection in a mirror.

She started talking as the bus pulled out of the station.

'They said Masses for the old people who are dead all over Ireland last week.

I keeps a Mass for them.

The Flemings and the Crossans blackguarded me when I lived in my two trailers.

I moved to another site and they still blackguarded me. Calling me names. Knocking on my trailer.

I was born and bred in Mitchel's Crescent, Tralee.

I bought a lovely raincoat in Killarney once but I never weared it.

My sister is acting sick. When I close my door there's no bell on it now.

Fuck off you city cunt, you dirty bollocks. How dare you speak to me like that.

Leanne Sheary spoke rotten like.

Do you think I'd forget the face of the worst enemy I ever had?

Goffo Geoghegan got ninety days in Cork Jail for not paying a fine of fourteen hundred euros for drunken driving.

At the trotting race in Ballybunion a shaft of a sulky went through one side of Flatpuss Finaghy's horse and came out the other side.

He drove another one up the Castlemaine Road, flogged it. The horse fell dead.

Chicken Slevin went out and got a rope and hung himself. It was out of badness. When there's something wrong it comes around. He said "It's small but there's more Irish in this than in all of you." I said "Stop showing yourself and pull up your trousers, you dirty fucking bastard. I have a brother and he'll mangle you.'"

She turned to me again with a vengeance.

'I see you admiring me shoes.

I do this at this time every night. For my arturitis.'

She took off her lemon-and-orange plimsolls and wrapped her foot in a page of *The Sun* with a photograph of a semi-nude mulatto girl with the finger tips over her breasts, wearing girdle held at thighs with rings, which revealed the shadow of her pubes.

A Traveller child like a stick of rhubarb with white-blond hair on top, periwinkle eyes, was repeatedly looking at his reflection like a blackbird looking at itself in a mirror.

His mother, like a fuchsine harem cushion with blonde hair on it, was on her mobile phone.

'I have to live too. I can't stay locked up in a trailer watching *Sponge Bob Square Pants* cartoons on television.'

A girl with crimson wet-dog-look hair started weeping loudly into her pink rabbit mobile phone with pink rabbit ears on it.

'My own Daddy will let me go home but my mother won't.'

And then the woman who looked like Maria Barbola got up and started screaming, her tantrum a crab-coloured explosion.

The bus stopped near Kilkera Old People's Home and an ambulance arrived.

Rivers run through County Limerick like lines through the palm of a hand.

The bus crossed two of them.

They'd brought Bishop Patrick Healy's body from Clonmel in 1647 to be buried by the Deel where there was a Franciscan Abbey and the Earl of Desmond's castle – he'd come ashore in July 1579 at Smerwick Harbour with the rebel against Elizabeth James Fitzgerald (who carried with him a papal brief to the effect that anyone who supported him would be granted a plenary indulgence and remission for their sins), was hanged in Kilmallock after being tortured, spikes driven through his fingers, some of which he lost, first Catholic prelate to be put to death since Henry VIII's break with Rome.

I'd lived in this place for three years after returning from England. It was as though there was an echo in the landscape at night that no one had patience with, a voice trying to tell you something, trying to tell you a story.

A robin is depicted pierced through the heart with an arrow in a stained-glass window at Buckland Rectory with its Welsh slate roof and Flemish garden wall under the Cotswolds, the oldest rectory in England, build around 1480 for the abbots of Gloucester with ashlar stone (squared blocks).

Robins built their nests in the torched cars by the Metal Bridge with a foundation of dead leaves, moss, lined them with hair, finished them off with a pigeon feather or a greenfinch feather.

'And so you cover your trail with leaves.

My hair turns in summer.'

It was all about segueing, the Metal Bridge, one thing leading to another, the way you make a stained-glass window of a boy with egg-yolk and copper-kettle hair, not in his monkey T-shirt, but in a T-shirt with the word Nagasaki and a sepia vision of the destruction of that city.

Walking through Truth Land

'No foot, no horse.'

A man with a face like a sea otter's speaking to a man with a ferocious red prophet's beard, like Ronnie Drew of the Dubliners.

A man like a grizzly bear with white flour thrown on his head makes an analogy.

'If you want to buy a bull, you judge him by the size of the balls.'

A passerby with head like a bullet with tomato-coloured cheeks takes up the point.

'I'm allergic to oranges. My balls are as big as them.'

He's referring to the orange in the grizzly bear's hand.

'The foal touches the bag and milk just comes pouring,' attests the sea otter who is wearing a Bronte-tweed flat cap.

'We'll split a hundred in Christ's name,' suggests Ronnie Drew.

'The truth is the truth is the truth!' cries out a man with a crutch, habit-brown ankle socks, who joins them.

'We're looking for sexy underwear,' a youth in pink singlet with carp face, like a carp with a shaven head, towing a girl with black-pudding stand up hairstyle, tells a Romanian woman in a Scheherazade dress – top red to breasts, then gold, blue and red pattern down its middle, oriental blue skirt with gold hemline.

The Romanian woman is selling dimensional pictures that shift image as you move yourself – Christ pointing to his heart that can become the Virgin Mary – a *Photoplay* cover girl (Mollie Ann Bourne, Mamie Van Doren) – who looks as if she's had a ghetto nervous breakdown.

Reading glasses. Hairpieces. Fretwork, many-coloured, collapsible planet playthings for children.

One Directions posters and transparent (other than picture) plastic shopping bags – the boys romping or showing their bird, rose, anchor, brigantine tattoos.

Ann Breen CDs with a sepia, photocopied cover of Ann Breen with clasp earrings, large American-style teeth.

On one side of the stall furniture with sex shop fuchsine upholstery.

On the other a cuisine that promises foot-long German sausages and chimney cakes.

Over all this – including framed pictures that give an illusion of depth (cross on right side, Ascension left, Flight into Egypt top, Crown of Thorns bottom, thumbnail Last Supper, Stable at Bethlehem, view of Jerusalem in corner niches) – Seamus Moore belts out: 'The old red flannel drawers that Maggie wore. They were tattered, they were torn.'

Paddy was a pye-dog wandering the road past the priory. A woman with two stub teeth, one on each side, wearing a raincoat she bought in Killarney for the first time, holds him on a leash.

'It's a holy place. But it's gorgeous,' she says about the priory.

It's like walking through a meadow of water forget-me-nots in the land given in frankalmoign – no obligation except praying – to the monks. It's like walking through the colour of someone's eyes you once knew. You keep expecting someone to say Hello but no one says Hello, and you think no-one is going to say Hello, until a boy with octopus roach, in a T-shirt with The Jetsons in an aerocar, who couldn't be more than thirteen, near the fourteenth-century bridge, says 'I'm twenty-seven. Say a poem.'

Baldy Cock Bracken bombed Bucko Bracken the other night. Drugs. Bucko makes his own false teeth. Baldy Cock swapped his trotting horse for two Jersey cows. There are millions of horses in South Hill. Fifteen boys got fifteen horses in O'Malley Park, put on balaclavas and smashed security cameras. Roane got a Dugy tattoo on the small of her back. That was her husband's name. But he said it was another Dugy. The one they met at a Swingers' Night at a sauna called Eye Candy. She went to a wedding and stayed all night. He cut the tattoo from the small of her back. He said he should have cut her eyes out and left them beside her.

I have an audience now of South Hill boys like weasel kits, one in a T-shirt with shark's face and wide open mouth, another in a T-shirt with nine posing ferrets, two of them French kissing, another in white T-shirt with Daffy Duck against a sepia lake with lots of mallards on it, another in T-shirt with headless gorilla, another in black T-shirt with spider's web on it, another in black T-shirt with fire brigade on it, another in white T-shirt with two grey pitbull dogs with flews, pink tongues showing and underneath Bow Wow Wow.

There's also a man in clove-and-cinnamon pinstripe suit, fly three-quarters the way down, with his sister's rose quartz wedding ring and a nineteenth-century watch from Amsterdam.

'He could be gay. He could be a child molester. We'll see him on BBC 3,' cautions a man with a head like a donkey's head with bald pate, donkey's grin among a group of youths with hair like saffron as a condiment sprinkled from the heavens, all in grey track suits which made them look as if they are wearing cement.

I recite W.B. Yeats' 'In Memory of Eva Gore-Booth and Con Markiewicz' and have to recite the part that demands a raised rhetorical voice for them on demand five times, each time earning a cheer as for a triumphant soccer conclusion and when I'm finished there's a mood swing – a revenge for the poem, a punishment for the light of evening at Lissadell, withdrawn pardon for the one condemned to death, execution on hindsight.

Three of the boys produce plastic pistols brought back from Lanzarote and start shooting at me with concentrated plastic pellets.

I hide behind a Range Rover with a trailer attached but a boy in a purple T-shirt with green dinosaur's death's head, sunglasses on the dinosaur's brow, eyes a historical blue – blue that used blot into the copybook once and he passes it on to my copybook (lessons about

the sacrifice of life in 1916 and the kneeling in the dust expected
for this at a school where women queued outside the classroom on
Fridays with Vincent de Paul vouchers) – shoots a pellet from behind
the trailer that hits me under the eye.

I take refuge among the amusements in a burdock field of derelict
sheds – the dodgems spin around to Ed Sheeran singing Rihanna's
'We Found Love'; there are Victorian galloping horses, fuchsine in
their cheeks, a train with carriages marked York, Normanton, Shef-
field, and a Jungle Adventure aerocastle with crimson bonobo (pygmy
chimpanzee) and green tiger on it – but the youths in trackie suits
like cement are on the premises.

'What is this poetry about?
Poetry isn't wanted here.'

I feel like the duck in Hook the Duck (anyone can be a winner).

I try to make a getaway from the town, heading in the direction
of the priory, where you could still see the string-course built to
prevent assault by weasels and martens, when a youth with urban fox
hair, locks, rodeo-denim blue eyes, in T-shirt with a tomcat's face and
the words Part Animal, stops me.

'Say that poem for me.'

I have to recite 'In Memory of Eva Gore-Booth and Con Markiewicz' to an audience of grey guinea fowl with white dots, khaki ducks,
Chiltern ducks, Welsh harlequin ducks, red mottled leghorn chickens,
white leghorn chickens in cages beside us, while One Direction sing
'Story of My Life', and a youth with hair the colour of a tribe of
apricots spiels his product – house cleaners.

I'd met him before on a Dublin street
'Are you looking for a hostel?' he asked me.
Shanno Sugruf was his name he said.
'I'll never set foot in Cork again.
Never or never is a long time.
I'm not going back to Cork. I'm not going back there. I'm not
going back to Cork.'
A borstal mark tear under right eye means bereavement.
A borstal mark tear under left eye means you've murdered someone.

He had a borstal mark tear under right eye.

To grow up with brothers writhing and wringing around one another like ferrets in a deep basket.

One of those brothers was knifed to death.

His sister who always made the pilgrimage to St Fanachan's Well in Mitchelstown on his feast day 25 November, in a Zhivago hat and fake mink coat, killed herself the same day.

Turn left at Tesco at the top of the top of the town. Brigtown Cemetery is on your right. You turn left at the crossroad to Mulberry. A raised footpath lined by old beech trees. Then you drink water from the well.

St Fanachan had a battle staff, the *Cenn Cathac* (Head Battler), which he carries in a statue of himself outside Mitchelstown Garda Station (he is sitting or crouching) in which he has the resigned look of one of the Mitchelstown guards.

St Fanachan asked seven tinsmiths to make seven sickles on which he mortified his body for seven years.

Bushes are cut along edges of fields for drainage in these parts and the felled bushes piled in the middle of the fields before being set on fire.

Shanno was not allowed out of Cork Jail for his brother's and sister's funeral but there were fires in the fields in his minds.

'Cork Jail is a shit hole. Pisspots wait until morning. To get water you fill your bottle and come back to the kettle in the cell.

You get to know a few fellows. You don't say you're this. You're that. You share the Munchies. Jelly popping candy shells and Cadbury Creme Eggs and Cadbury Bubblys and Cadbury Golden Biscuit Crunch.'

He showed me a white Portlaoise photo identity card.

'My family killed people and when I was put in Portlaoise a man from Togher, Gummy Gheeze – the only person there with no teeth – took me under his wing and protected me. Otherwise they'd have stuck a shaft in me because of my family.

When I was fourteen another Traveller boy of fourteen – The Pedlar they called him because him and his brothers would take copper and wire from newly built houses – stuck a bowie knife in my hip, ran it over, dented the hip bone. If I hadn't turned I'd be a dead man. He was aiming at my stomach. That happened on We the People Street.'

Shanno looked like a baby kangaroo with a hip-hop hair style then. He carried half a golf stick as a weapon and later a Stanley knife.'

Since that happened We the People Street has changed. The youth club paint the galvanized walls for Easter and Christmas.

There are pine trees now, a log hut with tied-back green curtains that have salmon trim, wine door with letter box.

There's a discarded black boot high heel and the pavement is strewn with cupcakes in baking cases.

Nearby Barnardo's Better Futures.

They are knocking houses down. There are metal fences and there is rubble.

A youth with outraged auburn hair, facial bruises that indicate some important nutrition is missing, is doing circles with a sulky in St Vincent's soccer field where a pizza delivery boy was recently dragged in and mangled.

Youth have hanged themselves on goalposts in Knocknaheeny. Maybe they've hanged themselves on this one. But it's not as bad as Tralee County Kerry.

In a house the colour of an armadillo to the Ascension Church side of St Vincent's soccer field – sixty years old, cross on top of it warding off the threat of industrial waste land owned by NAMA above it – with Kashmir-white geraniums outside it and a shrine with the Sacred Heart and the Blessed Virgin, both with hearts like blood octopuses, spider-leg tentacles around the hearts, she with a wreath of plastic dianthus, there's a photograph of seven Tralee youths, one kin – his hair and features have the gleamings of the liquid scarlet berry of the strawberry tree – against a goal post in Oatfield. Five attempted suicide on the goal post. Four succeeded, including their kin.

A bus with Lionel Ritchie's face blown up outside it and an Ava's icecream van goes by and I continue up the hill.

They had reunions at Gerry Whelan's pub in New Square in Mitchelstown, which was once a barracks, the boys who'd been in Cork Jail together. Shared cigarettes outside the pub, trackie bottoms pulled up like toreador trousers, pompons as big as dumb-bells on woollen caps.

(Shanno lifted a weight bar with car wheels on the end of it in Knocknaheeny. 'I'm like Scarface. All I have is my balls.' When Shanno's pubes were just coming, brick red like the knot's summer breast when he comes in August, those balls were objects to be handled by brothers who boxed in a boxing club in winter, wearing plum tomato-coloured boxing gloves, horse iodine all over the place because of all the blood, and a turf fire lighting and they all boxing around the fire. The extra-lean amber August fox, snowy face, ravishing black outlines – pared-down truth – who comes to steal the silver birch Japanese cocks and what they called silver fanny hens in the back garden, you learn something from this.)

And outside Gerry Whelan's pub Branchy, one of the boys who'd been in Cork Jail, would crouch like St Fanachan outside the Garda Station, ears of his white Afghan hat dangling, to receive the kisses of Cocoa, a mongrel terrier, brown as the body's recesses.

Lidl in Mitchelstown is the same as Lidl everywhere else but Cork Jail is different from other jails.

The circus animals are held in quarantine in England so Mary Chipperfield brought her circus to Spain. Her father came to visit her in a chopper.

Being in Cork Jail was like being a circus animal in quarantine in England.

Twenty-three hour lockdown padded cell in Mountjoy, on suicide watch, wearing nothing but black briefs with yellow lower hem and a pouch with ferret's face with two white eyes, before being sent to the committal prison of Portlaoise. That was after Cork Jail. And what did you think of? Branchy Kennevey who'd been in Cork Jail with him was from Fermoy, his family married into the Travellers at Castletownroche, and he'd told him how in Beechfield Cemetery during the Famine starving dogs – a dog for Shanno would always be his father's dog Mr Wrinkles, Australian shepherd and pit terrier, colour of night and a moon and a hamster, his father would take walking by the wood dock by the Lee – would dig up pauper's graves, the gravediggers not digging deep enough, coffins buried a few inches from the surface; the snuff porn – a man with bloodhound's face sprinkled with pepper, Messiah-length hair, in Knockaheeny videos his ten- and nine-year-old sons having sex and disseminated it and that was called snuff porn – that used happen in the lanes of the military part of town, Little England; about the black boy Jimmy Durham from Sudan, his mother killed on a boat in which she was taking him to Egypt when attacked by Durham Light Infantry, the Infantry taking him, christening him, eventually bringing him as a regimental bandsman to Fermoy where he died not much more than a boy, of pneumonia, his Fermoy grave marked by a white cross.

And about Pob Horken, a Traveller boy from Fermoy, still in Cork Jail, stud in his left ear, Mass wafer-white rosary around his neck, sides of his head like a shorn rabbit, altogether with the look of a Vincent's Workshops toy punished by many hands, listening to these stories in a tank top – Montano as Scarface on it with butt of cigar in mouth and the words Drugs Saved My Life – with ferret eyes.

Up from Cork with a mobile phone charger and twenty-five euros. Most of it spent on the first night's hostel.

Near Spar on Amiens Street.

'If I have to beg on the streets I will. I did in London.'

And he displayed a souvenir other than Portlaoise Jail identity card – stub of an Aer Lingus Heathrow ticket.

'There was a pile of horses on the commonage by Apple computers. The horses turned up the soil. They took everything. The Turleys don't even have a goat left.'

This hegira from Cork to Dublin would become hostels in Georgian houses like tomatoes Romanian women scavenged at the end of the day on Moore Street or Camden Street, no horses in his dreams in these hostels, only heartbroken zebras grazing.

'Stop shooting me,' he would say to the city where he would queue in Skipper's Lane by St Peter and Paul Church for the food parcels the Capuchins give out and where he would sit in a cafe with fire-brigade red seating, tiled fire-brigade red enclosure to fish and chip counter with a woman whose hair was as Canadian snow, around her neck a large roundel medal of Our Lady of Pompeii with Saint Catherine of Alexandria (from whose head milk flowed when she was beheaded, who appeared to Joan of Arc with a crown on her head) before he accompanied her, her hair surf-suds against the Liffey, she trailing her carry on, carrying some of her belongings in plastic bags, to a night refuge where in late summer she eats blackberries in a yogurt tub for her supper she's picked in the city suburbs.

Walking through Truth Land.

Looking for accommodation in this city was like cruising through Golgotha and it was on one of those days of looking – I'd seen a picture of Padre Pio stabbed on a hallstand and met a youth in Timberland boots (Shanno was wearing tan Caterpillar boots from Penneys) fleeing unsettled Moscow by that hallstand on a similar search – days of epileptic daffodils.

Becoming homeless suddenly is like having a bomb dropped on your life.

'Not fit for rats to live in,' the Moscow youth said about some mecca for silverfish he'd seen that day.

Looking for a room in this city was like a woman having an abortion.

'Where will I get a one bedroom flat in this murk?' said a woman in Argyle socks, white plimsolls, diamante hairband, bortsch-pink jacket, rose mittens with sky-blue lines in them sticking out of her jeans pocket, young but with a despairing orangutan's face, as she entwined herself deeper in the youth with heightenings in his jeans, with whom she was sharing a roll-up.

'I've a lot of worries. I'm going to walk into the Liffey. I'll drown,' a man whose legs wobbled like a grasshopper's so he looked like a grasshopper with copper hair, had avowed as he looked at a black guillemot on the Liffey, who had just turned black again after being white for winter, whom he was thinking of joining. Did he know that a dune-coloured rabbit, who likes flat parsley, of a man who'd been homeless for twenty-two years, from out there in Ballyfermot where the Gala Cinema is now Bingo, was flung in the Liffey near this spot and redeemed by his owner? 'Happy as Larry now,' says his owner in a deerstalker hat as the rabbit looks out inquisitively from the zip top of a carry on as the man's Pomeranian follows them.

Shanno had seen a black rabbit on his way from Cork to Dublin.

'We're a family of two and we're homeless,' a woman with Toby Jug countenance told me, paraffin-purple ribbon at back of her hair in crab smock, striped trackie bottoms, the only feminine thing a delicate leopard-spot scarf tied around her neck. Her teenage son beside her demonstrated his pink flushed leg – a shop girl's leg – in blue and suffering plimsolls by pulling up his trackie bottoms. Baby fringe. Adonis luxuriant mouth, facial features.

When they did have a home he was taught boxing at Frankie Kerr Memorial Hall Boxing Club in Drimnagh – where opposite Luigi's Fish and Chip Place and Pizzeria two Polish youth were asked to buy drink from an off-licence for underage drinkers, refused, screwdriver driven in one of their heads, the other jumped off a crane from grief – by Michael Carruth, Barcelona Olympic boxing champion, masseur to the Westmeath Football team, from a Protestant North of Ireland family who became Dublin Catholics, great granduncle executed on Republican side in the Civil War.

'My nose has been broken so many times I don't notice,' said Shanno showing me a photograph of Conor 'Notorious' McGregor, mixed martial-arts artist – boxing, kickboxing, Brazilian Jiu Jitsu, capoeira – wearing only leather briefs, with the Tricolour draped on his shoulders.

He'd wait in Dublin until he saw Conor McGregor oppose Cole Miller in the UFC fight in mid July.

In Knocknaheeny Shanno would box wearing nothing but faux lion-skin briefs and then have a Breast in a Bun meal from Burger Hut.

To beg I am not ashamed. He did it before when he lived with father, Savage, eyes the colour of gravestones, in Milford Estate, near Surrey Docks. There was a black dealer there called Elephant. 'What do you expect me to do?' Savage had asked Social Welfare, 'Swim back to Knocknaheeny? Swim back to The Glen? Swim back to St Lukes? Swim back to Blackpool Shopping Centre?' Savage died of a heroin overdose. 'If God wants you, he will call you.' Elephant gave up dealing and started a house church in Milford Estate at the same time. 'I was convicted in my soul.'

Del Del his mother, dirt on the street Shanno said, sex for the crack.

A woman like a Samurai wrestler walked past us, cigarette like rocket in each ear.

Del Del goes begging with a foxy long-haired chihuahua Little Ted, as she leads a blind man, Eyeball Furney, who wears a sombrero.

You'd see them near Heckscher (suppliers to the piano trade since 1883) in Kentish Town or New Camden Chapel Methodists Church with its two pillars or the yellow and green brick Hope & Anchor pub on Crowndale Road or situating themselves under the George's flag somewhere, she a woman with high forehead, cleft bald spot at the back of head, algal — hanging grooves — in face, like stalactites, often in a fudge-pink flared trousers.

She called you Baby until you were six or seven in Knocknaheeny, dressing you in a cinnamon suit like a prince.

Taking the 202 bus to Knocknaheeny is like being in the Armageddon of a courthouse, faces colours of Dracula make-up, blue, purple, red. A gallery of prison tattoos. Perhaps it's like being in Portlaoise Jail.

He wasn't afraid of death Shanno told me. He was afraid of being a vegetable in a wheelchair. Showed me the meat-cleaver scar on his forehead.

Four gangs after one gang. They come up from Togher.

'They're *jalous*.'

He and his brothers had a Wembly .22-calibre revolver. 9mm automatic handgun, a Beretta.25, a .38 revolver, a .12 gauge shotgun, a Smith and Weston Full rifle, a 2.2 rifle, a sawn-off Beretta rifle.

There'd been shots through the window. He was afraid to go into the back garden where the silver birch Japanese cocks were.

In his mind it was all like when Skigger, a cousin of theirs, roach like a Khepresh, a Pharoah's war crown, was chased by a squad car out the South Ring by-pass tunnel, went up an embankment, was killed.

The story of my life on a Dublin street where a girl in fuchsine jump suit passed – in this city of herring gulls who approach those sleeping out as if they are smoked haddock on sale, of kestrels in belfrys, of guillemots on suicide water (eight and a half thousand people had disappeared in the country in the past year a man with facial growth the colour of Lucozade, in Smartie-red jacket on a bus coming into the city had told me, leaning his head back on the seat like an apostle, many left the country, many committed suicide) – like a flamingo on crutches.

Lego, Shanno's oldest brother had died in his sleep aged forty-nine.

'Nine yards in and out,' he'd said about the farm-school he's been sent to in Cork after being caught shoplifting. Thirteen. Shared a room with a sixteen-year-old. But then you're spoken for, matched at a very early age with a Traveller girl, married in St Mary's Cathedral, The North Chapel.

'Go in there and say a few prayers for Lego.'

Young, Lego had an Adonis roach with frontal spare rat-tails. Ash Wednesday-ash moustache, cigarette periodically put in his mouth not so much to smoke as a habit of show, as saying he welcomed attention.

When he died he was a man with a hare lip who looked as if part of his face was chewed away by the dog that leaped off Dracula's ship.

Lego's coffin was borne in a black, gilded-edge funeral hearse coach drawn by two cream draught horses, the kind the guards use, but with white plumes, the driver all in black, but not in a top hat, but black homburg hat, the coach covered with teddybears, horse-shoe wreathes, bird-cages trussed with flowers, past Key Cabs and Mahony's (minerals, tobacco, newsagents, top ups), past St Vincent's soccer field where a sulky doing circles was followed by a black grey-hound and an indeterminate hound, girls behind in hoop earrings and diamante belts like the gold and silver of Montezuma that Spain seized from Mexico, to St Mary on the Hill Church.

Outside it a woman in Capuchin friar type raingear, was heard to say: 'They eat too much. They drink too much. They smoke too much. They have sex too much and they don't take exercise.'

At the top of the hill, past the flanks of fawn, mauve, grey, terra-cotta, emerald, bottle green houses, past the industrial waste land owned by NAMA, past the reservoir with one skewbald horse, soiled like a turnip just picked from the ground, left after the confiscations, is a shrine with a statue of the Blessed Virgin and the Sacred Heart, two kneeling angels, both with their heads chopped off, an empty Green Giant corn-on-the-cob tin thrown on it, the kind of memorial shrine Lego will have, a halting site nearby, a field with empty gas canisters and lopsided horse boxes between the halting site and the shrine, where a mallard and his wife live, far from water.

Looking down at Cork from here is like looking down at it from space or from Heaven.

Down there in Cork there are some who believe that there are people who live in Knocknaheeny who dognap small domestic dogs – shnauzers, shih-tzus, crested Chinese, Lhasa Apsos, Tibetan terriers, Japanese chin dogs, Boston terriers, Mexican hairless dogs, West Highland terriers, French bulldogs – and throw them to wild Rottweilers in Knocknaheeny for bets and then set the Rottweilers on one another.

One woman who dresses in dignified black from head to foot, black cloche hat, except she wears Clube de Ragatas de Flamengo scarlet-and-black stripe soccer stockings, claims Gisela her daschund puppy perished in this way.

'I'm a Traveller,' Shanno tells everyone he meets to extricate himself, to save his history and his family history – his family used go to Spilsby in Lincolnshire once from Cork for potato picking, the fasten penny contract for autumn and winter work, Hogmanay more celebrated than Christmas because the bosses were Scottish, Scotland the coldest country in the world it was said and the Cork Traveller women marrying into the Scottish Travellers who were always drinkers and who had their own ways and the Cork women having to adapt to them but now they say there's a new generation – from the colour pink that is the colour of poverty.

A rose-pink blanket with white rabbit heads over a mulatto baby, his white mother holding pink purse with galaxy scintillation, her hair pink-sienna.

Dirty purple, plum, claret anoraks.

Over another baby a powder-red blanket with aquamarine owl heads on it.

Amid the reds there's a child's forget-me-not blue eyes in home-less seagull-featured face.

Another small boy with light ginger hair, front tooth missing, dabs of ointment snow over his face, in lemon and orange plimsolls, says 'I'm ringing my nanny.'

Walking through Truth Land and who did you meet?

A man who stands on Nicholas Street beside Christ Church Square all day, opposite St Audoen's Catholic Church from which Poles steal candles and boil kettles on them, black woollen hat pulled down on his face that greatly resembles that of early Abbey actor Barry Fitzgerald, extra large carry on beside him, bags, wears a black rain cape that makes him look like a Connaught nun, but when summer comes closer – and the blue geraniums and black mullein planted by a gardener who died suddenly after planting them intermingle in St Audoen's medieval church where Margaret Ball thrown into a dungeon by her own son for not taking the Oath, is buried – and the date of the Conor McGregor and Cole Miller fight (you did Thai boxing and main boxing yourself) draws nearer, wears true white plimsolls and you can see his tie, white tie, interlocking signal-red-and-black bar patterns.

He takes notes.

'I'm watching the traffic until five.'

'Why don't you sit down?'

'Bring me an armchair.'

King Shanno is running wild.

With his hair colour Shanno through Dublin like a cardinal bird let loose in the streets.

Bearberries grow where the Sugruf Traveller king's horses, banshee-white and lavish-haired, graze and fleabane outside the cemetery where he is buried.

On the Sugruf king's grave, with its blooded marble cross, is a tall Blessed Virgin in white and blue, her teenage son to left side, in azure garments, pointing to his heart, peony-size rose in left hand, his hair curly Titian-red of the Sugrufs.

Criminal, convict, prisoner, beggar: but the part of you they didn't get hold of has royal blood, is a King; in such a cosmogony you had ancestors who were kings before Christ healed the ten men who were lepers.

Such cosmogonies help you to walk through Truth Land. They sit beside you when you are a pariah dining at Morelli's, established 1959, or Iskander's kebab house — shawarma specialist (marinated slices of lamb, chicken built up) – or Aussie-outback BBQs.

'Brother.'

The sores on a junkie's face outside Good World Restaurant are as big as lollipops; Tinker's, Traveller's facial features once, auburn colouring still in the hair, the features having become amorphous – they are not adrift from tribe, they have excommunicated themselves from Tribe.

'O the streets of Dublin city can be friendly and so bright

But somehow seems so lonely to strangers in the night.'

Big Tom blasts from a white Traveller van with bars on top, which looks like an argument, a fight, a stoush, and you wonder are these Royal Kin?

To follow the seal up the Lee to the Swimming Hell Hole as he looks for salmon. You can't eat raw fish. You need other sustenance — Morelli's, established 1959, Iskander's kebab house, Aussie-outback BBQs. To follow the seal down river, as he snortles like a king, disturbing herons who complain like lags, his belly full.

But the river is not his Kingdom. His realms are when he reaches the salt tide, past the salmon pass and the half barrier to one side of the middle bank. This place is not your Kingdom, will never be your Kingdom.

When my father died first to greet me outside the church was Bridie Lawrence, a Traveller woman – thin as an eel, sharp featured as an axe, hair in two separate strands, sockets in her face, in someone's cast-off chin-up coat – with her fracture of sons with true fox-sedge hair.

I went almost immediately afterwards to Lissadell Beach below Lissadell House with a friend, a guard from County Kerry. Forget the pain and remember the flowers he liked to say.

It was the tall goldenrod, the autumn hawkbit, the water-forget-me-nots, the Japanese knotweed, the Russian vine, the toadflax that day. Toadflax used be used for dropsy. The hemp agrimony had turned to banks of fluff like mattresses slashed to pieces.

When I was a child my father had taken me to a summer magic-lantern performance of *Twelfth Night* in the Greek Temple on the lake in Blackrock Park where the rudbeckias, the coneflowers, thrive until late November.

'Not a flower, not a flower, sweet

On my black coffin let there be strewn.'

The barnacle geese had already arrived in Goose Field and sounded like a pack of dogs.

My mother had given me my father's gold stretchy band watch.

'Here, wear this jewel for me ...'

I'd left it on the beach with my clothes when I went swimming and a mist and late October darkness came and I couldn't find the watch with my clothes and I searched for an hour or two, in the dark, on my knees, sifting and flaying the sand, until I found it and I held it in my hand and I held his stories of rebellion and civil war, and to forget the pain the water-forget-me-not river.

Famine Rain

I remember the poor people, the very poor of my childhood, women in scarves, St Vincent de Paul coats, bent over a little.

A woman in a scarf patterned with oatmeal and piebald sows and coat with black collar and black belt, black-outlined white squares, blue-and-red moiré effect around the squares, crossing the understory of holly in the Black Woods with a black pram before Christmas to collect wood.

When berries were hanging from the trees she'd say it was a sign of a bad winter. There to feed the birds. The greenfinches knew when it is going to snow. Like the ones who head into town on Saturday nights and hang around Swanwick's Cinema.

King Alfred's cakes black fungus on the trees in the Black Woods. The flowering quince — Japanese quince trees — with red berry broken out in three glowing orange seeds, with a crown of five tiny pale petals.

Hazel wood for charcoal on which you could grill a rabbit caught by her son with a shaven head like a golf ball with pepper shaken on it.

When I was a child and all the Christmas cards would be in — Nativity scenes in Guinness colours, snow-covered villages against coffee backgrounds — and the nomenclature gone through, there would be an inventory of those who hadn't written, an inventory of absences. A Christmas-card lacuna often meant a grave in England.

Babycham for the eldest and a card from last year with a Golden Dome view of Jerusalem recalled:

'Came over in 1959. I was twelve-and-a-half years old. They couldn't understand a word I said and they still can't. If you want to lose your accent you'll lose it. If you don't you won't.

28 July coming. The couple next door, man and wife, look after me.'

Eyebrows that leapt from his face. Smoked Players.

'You have no luggage,' it was remarked on his last visit.

'What need have I of luggage? I have two houses. One in Glasson. One in Bradford.'

I had no luggage when I was rushed by ambulance to hospital in bicycle reflector jacket, black T-shirt, Addicted shorts from Vincent's.

It was just before Christmas. A cafetiere broke in my hands as I was washing it after breakfast and a chunk of Pyrex nearly severed my right thumb.

Hunky Dorys Buffalo & Salt and Salt & Vinegar, Tayto Snax, Toffee Twist, Moro Twirl in a dispensing machine: two Down Syndrome teenage boys getting Velvet Crunch Spring Onion and Cheddar Cheese and Tayto Cheese & Onion from the machine.

One with eyes like the pebbles one puts in a snowman in Noddy beanie and T-shirt with word Happy, doodle face with tiny legs under it pulling a smile with fists, the other with tow-headed raspberry face with acne, in T-shirt with a collage of black-and-white images from the vampire series *True Blood*.

'I'm from the Dead Centre of Dublin,' the second one tells me. 'Glasnevin. Where the dead are buried.'

The trolley lady, in dolly-blue smock, with hair a snakes and ladders of red, crimson, alizarin, pink, passes, singing 'The Cowboy's Lament' ... 'Bury me out on the prairie,' and a woman with roller-coaster brows, eyelashes colour of plastic greenery, black shrubs at the ends of them, lower lip purple above, red below, stretch-limousine nails colour of Walt Disney snow, crawls on the ground.

Daros is from Lanzarote. Wears a baseball hat with the three railway engines (Edward, Gordon, Henry) at the front, which is turned back to front, and a wraparound scarf.

Met Irish tourists in the hotel he was working in. Wanted to come to Ireland. His parents from Galicia. In Ireland for two years. Row with his girlfriend who has stand-up hair like a Galway sausage (jumbo black sausages) 5 am. Beat walls with fists. Broke two knuckles in right hand. Fractured wrist.

'You may never be able to use your right hand again,' the young doctor in shearling jersey, chocolate-leather shoes and berry-red socks, tells me the evening before my operation.

The youth in the next bed, with blond kraut (Prussian sauerkraut) hairstyle and eyes blue as urban forget-me-nots, pale blue of a Penal Days Madonna, himself in pale-blue pyjamas, had given me a pair of pale-blue Penneys pyjamas and a scarlet Liverpool toothbrush, both supplied to him by his foster mother. Naty he said his name was. Voice that came from the grimalkin roads, cottages with Jacob's Ladder outside them, tea roses hanging like the laden part of a weighing-scales, fuchsia bushes shaped like boxing gloves, silvery, emerald, sad cerulean countryside with a grotto of Mary where the statue had been abducted but where people still left flowers, but also from the violent urban eruptions of poppies.

Punched, held down, his neck stomped on the previous Saturday night under the beech trees outside Kilkenny Castle by a bed of black-mouth Mamba serpent boys from New Park estate (their hoodie uniforms and in most cases their hair like the blackened inside to mouth of that deadly serpent).

Had been forewarned by their voices that carried on the smell of chips like the sound of alouattes – howling monkeys – from outside Marble City Grill and Roma Café. These boys always stopped on

John's Bridge as they crossed it to spit, like the Mozambique spitting cobra, at the mallards.

Naty recognized one of them, The Rover, a youth like a mandrake plucked from the ground wearing glasses, hoodie on his head like a nun's veil, face white as Ferryhouse Industrial School bread, forehead fringed by mini-sausage size bangs, as he stood over him.

'You give me the creeps,' The Rover had hollered into the Kilkenny night in which girls walked like Shetland ponies in hot pants and black leggings and a Stag party group wandered with photographs of themselves in their underwear superimposed on the front of their black jerseys.

They took his link card, mobile phone, a watch with leopard-spot face that had belonged to his dead mother.

Jaw broke, he'd have to wear a pin and plate for life.

Jealous they were of his prowess with Texas Hold 'Em and Omaha at The Pussycat Casino.

Jealous of how Lol Butter the drag queen who'd come to sing and dance at the hen party and who'd arrived at The Pussycat Casino in a hummer limousine, wearing a pink marshmallow hat, black dress with fox fluff at the shoulders, red polka-dot pendant earrings, had taken his hand as Dada and Sandy Riviera sang 'Lollipop' – 'If I lick your ice-cream you can lick my lollipop.'

On Naty's chest were tattooed the words: 'Miss you and would give anything to have you back,' underneath the word Blessed with a swallow on either side; under the nape of his neck a Death's Head leprechaun with cigar in mouth from Swine Line in Waterford; on his right arm a very recent tattoo in memory of Jacintha Sald-hana, the Indian nurse who'd worked in England for ten years and committed suicide in King Edward VII Hospital after she'd answered the telephone to two Australian DJs impersonating royalty, who were enquiring about the Duchess of Cambridge, currently under observation in the hospital – three roses flanking blue hearts with a rosary alongside; at the bottom of his right leg was his mother's name Kelsey; at the bottom of his left leg a lizard on its back that he got in Lanzarote for 120 euros. He said he'd never get a tattoo in Lanzarote again because the tattoo was lopsided – crooked.

'That young fellow will have no toothbrush for himself,' a woman whose hair was a blonde porridge, had shrimp-pink nail varnish, was sitting by the bed of her husband, who had an Arsenal tattoo To Do Is To Dare, and vintage Johnny Eagle tattoos, a Death's Head wearing an opera hat – The Duke, and a Death's Head with a lion's mane over the Irish tricolor, had said sharply to me when Naty had given me the pyjamas and toothbrush. They'd just made a presentation of a box of Quality Street with Regency ladies with cottage bonnets on it, to a nurse with a tan from the Greek isle of Zakynthos.

Naty told me a toothbrush story, the first of many stories he told me that night.

With the money he won at The Pussycat Casino he would buy take-aways from Supermac's or Subway or Eddie Rocket's or Apache Pizza for poor Travellers or walk out to the Halting Site by Ciaran's Cemetery or the one at White Bridge on the Callan Road or to the Wetlands where a mother locks herself in a room when the sons return from the pub, ('They rape the daughters. One of them raped his four-year-old son'), with clothes in black Jack and Jones bags.

Topper lives in the Wetlands. 'He's only that size.' His parents abandoned him when he was six years old. Father thought he was the child of someone else. But he was the only one who looked like his father. His brothers didn't look like their father. Grandmother and Grandfather on Colinn Hill looked after him.

'Travellers are bloodlines.'

No toothbrush until he was eleven.

'You have to give childer a toothbrush,' Topper would say. 'Gums get bad.'

His grandfather gave him a few tips. His uncle used to beat him for stealing jelly teddybears and fizzy lollies and mini choc eggs.

His mother died in Berlin. Schönfield Holiday Camp near airport. Father still there.

He'd go and visit them.

His mother had a Central Asian Shepherd dog called Buddy.

He went to the dog races at Lankwitz.

He liked the kugel cake with red currants and learnt some German: 'Das thut gut.'

Winters cold in Berlin, end of winter still cold. Hitler's death announced midnight Mayday and it was snowing.

Grandmother died in her seventies. Grandfather at eighty-six.

'I'm into friendship with the three creators,' Topper would say. 'Father, Son, and Holy Ghost.'

'Where does the tide go when it goes out to sea? It must go somewhere.'

He had a Nigerian friend who had a house in Dublin 2 with whom he sometimes stayed, taking the bus from MacDonagh Station beside Eddie Rocket's with no baggage, in just a black T-shirt with four little green soldiers in First World War-type helmets taking a salute, watched by a green superior.

Topper's favourite song that he'd sing on the journey to Dublin was Karen Carpenter's 'I'll Say Goodbye to Love'... 'No-one ever cared if I should live or die.'

Small like a circus seal and walked like one. Victim of malnutrition as a child. Circus seal with auburn hair or a penguin, a penguin who didn't have a toothbrush as a child.

Naty in his pale-blue pyjamas with his dirty-blond hair, body spare like a cheap hotel, colour of white dead nettle, boxer's arms like osiers, boy denuded like the poplars, chestnut trees, beeches, ash trees, alders by the Old Weir in December, was like one of the ikon makers in the Adriatic post of Ravenna in the sixth century who composed their ikons, their stories with stone, glass cubes – picking the stones – against backgrounds of fragments of jaundiced glass. Sometimes a lengthy caesura between the stones. The Christ featured in these ikons was a beardless youth, almost a teenager. Teenagers have hung themselves from the trees by the Old Weir.

'Salmon come up from the sea December and January to spawn. By canal walk. Cross the Old Weir. Spawn on shallow, rocky parts of river.

You buy red maggots from Froggy Fresh beside Green's Bridge. Four doors down.

The river is fished out. Once you'd catch sixteen pounders. Now you catch two or three pounders. Sprats.

They were dredging the Nore because salmon couldn't get through near canal, beside castle, throwing manikins in to test. "That's not a manikin," someone shouted. "That's a body!"

Face to bank. A suicide.'

There'd been a manikin in one of the antique-shop windows on John Street day of his mother's funeral, a manikin with fox eyebrows, fox walrus moustache, fishing rod in hand, swilling Guinness with other hand, his trousers falling down, leprechaun-green shirt, pocket hand-kerchief, turtle Fair Isle socks showing.

An ensemble of mallards set sail as the hearse crossed John's Bridge where a fracture of backsides in Dunnes Stores, check boxers show when the New Park boys lean over, not Justin Bieber's after-the-show buttock-clinging designer briefs. To find Justin Bieber under-wear you have to win and win heavily at The Pussycat Casino.

His eyes had never been bluer as he walked behind the hearse past O'Reilly's Hardware (cane furniture, wedding gifts, pictures, mirrors) who rent out rooms in houses to which Polish salesmen with pony-tails call.

Mormon-boy eyes, lost-boy eyes – Mormon boys excommu-nicated, persuaded to leave when they reach their teens because they are competition in a polygynous community where there are too few women, pretext, excuse maybe being they watched a movie, TV, played football, talked to a girl, and being well built, like the Nephilim who married daughters of men, who made those around them look like grasshoppers, because Mormon life is an outdoor life, drift into prostitution or porn films in LA, having obtained fake IDs.

The hearse passed Muscle Nutrition Ireland – a demi-model outside with strawberry-coulis nipple, parchment tan – the model looked as if his skin was made from cornflakes.

Naty had seen himself reflected in a Fry's Chocolate mirror, by appointment to H.M. The King and Queen, on a cold March day in a white, open-necked shirt and seriously tailored trousers.

Loreena, his sister – half-sister, child of a man from Tilbury, Essex – had dyed her hair crimson for the funeral so she looked like a Walt Disney witch, walking behind the hearse in a town of witches, witches wearing birds' masks, leading greyhounds with ash-and-turquoise streamers, sad witches with sad demons in cap and bells, retreating in the rain over John's Bridge after the St Patrick's Day Parade.

Alice Kyteler, the Kilkenny witch, had a bit part in Irish history, for which she'd dressed up like one of the drag queens in dresses with word patterns, like Hold Me Baby, black dresses with scarlet letters appliqued all over them, leopard-spot dresses, galazy mini-dresses, flamingo boas, red, blue, yellow costume jewellery.

'To the house of William my sonne
Hie all the wealth of Kilkennie town.'

Naty's stepfather from Tilbury wore a Marks and Spencer suit and tie for the funeral, not a black tie, but a tie with a nine-to-five pattern.

'I know you lost your mother,' he said to Naty. 'I lost her too. We lose for fuck's sake.'

A young Pakistani man in Santa Claus beanie and white coat poured Naty a cup of trolley-service coffee.

'Went back to Pakistan October for one month. I'm engaged. Returning in a month to marry. No sex before marriage. I'm not as young as I look. It's time to settle down.'

Naty told a Christmas story his grandfather – Adolf moustache, front bottom tooth forgone – who looked after him initially as his mother was too young to look after him, had told him.

Christmas Eve 1950 – when the Travellers had pulled in for the winter to The Butts by Old Canice's Hospital in Newry bow-top wagons – ('My mother had geese then and the geese were laying early and the Tinkers were always looking for goose eggs. A Tinker is not afraid of any dog in Christendom but is terrified of geese. They'd rather take on one of the swans that nest by the Nore in winter than a goose. When the geese would hiss they'd go') – his mother was looking out the window in Kilkenny and she suddenly saw his father coming up Wolfe Tone Street. Home from the British army in Manchester. She flew up the street and bought a turkey in Irishtown.

His brother came up to him in the middle of the night with a present his father had brought.

A red train with a grey face you wound up.

His brother – eyes the blue that was inside the marbles with which he'd played on the streets of Kilkenny – went over to Manchester and joined the British army with his father. He was sent to Malaya where he died of malaria.

And then another story of his grandfather's – who had an Australian hat with a green piper's plume he wore for 1798 re-enactments and who was always playing Paul Robson singing Kevin Barry on a 78.

He used to go to a farmhouse like an ivy Pomeranian outside Kilkenny with a manna ash tree growing by its wall, for milk.

It was near the rag tree.

An arson's cottage opposite. (His word for artisan.)

The fountain butterfly bush, the weeping buddleia, the weeping tree growing in the front garden.

Mother died in childbirth Christmas Day. Girl came to mind four brothers.

Father had sex with the girl. Priest scandalized and brothers sent to orphanages. All different. Glin. Greenmount and Upton in Cork. Ferryhouse, Clonmel.

He went to a funeral in the farmhouse and spoke to the lady who'd moved into the artisan cottage.

She heard the young man's voice outside one day saying: 'That's the window of the room I used sleep in.'

She asked the young man, who had hair like diced carrot, and his wife – in her moss-green jump suit and her petal-satin lipstick she looked like Jill St John whom you'd see at the Regent on William Street – in for tea and gur cake (everything was in the larder for weeks in the cake).

They'd married in Quix Road Catholic Church in Kilburn and they lived in Quix Road.

The young man said he knew one brother was dead, but not

before he'd heard the horse-like yaffle of the green woodpecker near Fiddler's Ferry Powerhouse between Widnes and Warrington, but the other brothers had disappeared without trace – rags on the rag tree.

And then they went on to the rag tree.

Lime tree one hundred years old. Pollarded. Collared trunk. Epicuticular – waxy – growth. Greyish bark. Red tints to big buds.

And what do you find at the rag tree?

Mother of Carmel scapulars. Tea towels. Reflector Christmas decorations. Rosary beads. Handkerchiefs. Over gloves. Insoles. Key bands. Loom bands. Crochet work. Blue, red, lavender, yellow, lemon strips. (As the strip rots an illness disappears or a wish comes true.) Terracotta pots under it with memorial cards in them, many of them young people.

The rag tree, the crann tree, the cloutie tree, the shamanic tree, the rainbow tree.

Travellers leave pictures at a halting site where a relative perished, bits of cloth, rags.

We hang our hopes, we hang our shortcomings, we hang our past, we hang our future. We hang the generations, we hang rags the blue of Mary who survived the Penal Days, we hang our messages to the dead. And maybe the rag tree will someday become a mustard tree.

After the funeral – the countryside an argument, a fracas of black-thorn blossom – Naty and Loreena went to the rag tree and hung a flash-scarlet kimono of their mother's that had humming birds, lotus flowers, subhas (Islam prayer beads) of white flowers on it.

'How old are meteorites?' Naty asked. 'She was always going over and reading her stars in Kilkenny. People who knew her at Itchy Coo Park Nightclub (who-hit-who Nightclub) said she was hyper.

The Social Worker told me my father is dead. If I met him I'd kill him.'

Hair that was basically Venetian blond but frequently dyed burgundy, pink, blue, green, yellow, sometimes with kipunjii (long-tailed Tanzanian monkey with crest of erect hair) Mohawk.

'He dyes his hair pink, blue, and every fucking thing. A fucking eejit, I swear to God,' a youth with mullet-attempt hairstyle, mustard, ginger and sausage hair and complexion, jeans drooping to show briefs patterned with yellow Christmas trees, said of Naty outside a tattoo shop with Popeye outside with dice, anchor, stars tattoos as if he had just come out of prison.

A large proportion of the town has been in Portlaoise Jail and is proud to show the white photo-identity card of Portlaoise Jail as if it is a Trinity College card.

'Fred Tiedt was a beautiful boxer my grandfather told me. His father emigrated from Germany. He won a silver medal in the 1956 Olympics in Melbourne. Used to box with Ski Mullen.'

Christmas when Zaconey American Spirit and West Coast Cooler & Vodka is drunk at the stag parties they play strip poker in the gaffs, lose a round and you remove an article of Jack and Jones clothing, reveal pubes the colour of yesterday's Lucozade. Naked, some of the New Park boys look like baby alligators fried in batter.

Naty's foster-mother – a woman with a floss of raven hair who, when she was going out, wore sunglasses and black mini-skirts and lace-up boot high heels and did her face up with malachite eyeshadow and peach-meringue lipstick – always painted a snowman with a sprig on his head on the window at Christmas, three pebble buttons, a lascivious grin, and a blonde girl in blue slit-dress waltzing.

His grandfather – he wore a pioneer pin and always went to the Pioneer Total Abstinence Association Annual General meeting at the Gresham Hotel in Dublin after Mass at the Pro-Cathedral – told him how the Kilkenny knights retreating from the Crusades removed the body of St Nicholas – who as a baby refused his mother's milk on Wednesdays and Fridays – from Myra and reburied him by the Nore in Kilkenny, marking his grave with a broken slab with a carving of a monk on it, and who, because of the custom of giving presents on his feastday in December that Dutch Protestants brought to New Amsterdam, became Santa Claus.

And after he was sent to his foster-mother because his grandfather could no longer look after him, and after he'd been in Dublin for a day if he'd taken the train, not the bus, Christmas decorations on the arched casement windows of Heuston Station, going home was going home to homelessness, going home to be an orphan, going home to a surrogate family, a surrogate Christmas, surrogate chintz.

When will kill this surrogate chintz in us I thought as a mobile phone went off in the hospital ward with the sound of Chris Rea singing 'Driving Home for Christmas'?

Little red-and-blue lights twinkled on the Christmas tree in my father's drapery shop window, there were silver bells on it and copper reflector balls with red threads and purple acrylic jewels on them. A crimson tinsel streamer was wound through the tree. On top was a lopsided saffron star – it looked as if it had just been to Ryan's Pub.

He met her last Christmas in London, she'd been staying in a woman's hostel in Kentish Town and she gave him a print, 'Life is a journey and love makes the journey worthwhile,' in black-and-red lettering on an ivory background, in Danny's Fish & Chips.

There'd been a homeless woman camping outside St Michael's Church on Camden Road who had a book about Naples on display beside her shiralee of bags and who systematically ate Kingsmill soft white sliced bread.

Loreena had returned from Tilbury a few years before with an Essex accent and worked in a bookies in Kilkenny where men in baseball caps stared hopefully at plasma television.

She had a boyfriend called Rabbit who looked like a rabbit with glistening blond hair in a track suit.

When they were both small children and Kelsey and Loreena were back on holiday in Kilkenny Kelsey had a large portrait of Naty and his sister done by an amateur painter, he presented with a lot of Prussian blue and bottle green, Loreena in flesh-colours, honey-yellows. Loreena wore sky-blue earrings.

Kelsey got a cherry-coloured frame for it at Liffey Craft in Dublin and the painting hung at his grandfather's house in Kilkenny.

'My ambition before I die is to play in Horseshow Casino in Las Vegas,' said Naty, 'and I want to be like Clint Eastwood.'

His father did pictures in charcoal. Elvis. Paul Newman. Clint Eastwood. Eastwood was young then.

The Yanks knew these people and he put his drawings up outside the National Portrait Gallery. He'd rub the charcoal with his fingers. He charged three pounds but the Yanks often didn't have the change and he'd get five pounds for the pictures he did of them.

The police never interfered with him. He'd be gone too quickly.

He'd go to the Galtymore in Kilburn and just sit there sketching and women like Kelsey would just come up to him. He was a member of the Workers Revolutionary Party. Did courses in Derby. He went to the United States. San Francisco.

Kelsey wanted to have an abortion but she saw the poster by Christ Apostolic Church in Kentish Town.

'I set before you Life and Death … that you and your descendants may live. DT. Choose life. I'm a child not a choice. Human life at eight weeks (two months).'

Child not a choice.

A hurley is a symbol of belonging in County Kilkenny. Young teenage boys carry hurleys like scepters through the town of Kilkenny. Young teenagers from Southern Sudan, fresh from Uganda, where they've been living, carry hurleys through the streets. What if you don't belong? What if you belong nowhere?

Kelsey returned to Kilkenny for a few years where she had a Russian boyfriend like a garden of sunflowers, who was deported. Knocked out her front tooth before being deported.

'He crushed me, he changed my personality.'

'There are 365 days in the year,' she said, before returning to live in England. 'If I have to live the rest of my days by myself I will.'

In her last autumn Kelsey hung around the garden of St Anne's in Soho with its oleanders, bay trees, London planes, limes, Chinese maples, one turned red because it got more sun.

With the colour of her hair she had a crimson wet-dog look over her square jaws.

'I've been all over England,' she told Naty when she met him in Danny's Fish & Chips at Christmas, 'Liverpool twice.'

It was when the honey locust trees were coming into leaf in Pimlico and the white winter violets were in full blossom in Soho Square Gardens – Naty had his hair in Liberty Spikes then (spare, individual spikes created with glue) – that Kelsey began having the hallucinations that led to her accident.

When she was a child her father had hired a woman hackney driver – who with her Shirley Temple blonde-gold clump of hair, her fuchsine cheeks, her Baby Face Nelson lips, her triple chins, her fuchsine cardigan, her extended stomach in a white cardigan, her dark-chocolate leggings, looked like a fuchsine apple – to drive them both to Shanrahan Cemetery near Clogheen, South Tipperary, in her Austin-Rover – the red sandstone Galtees to the north and the Knockmealdowns to the east – where Father Nicholas Sheehy is buried.

Educated in Louvain, ordained in Rome, when Ireland was racked by Famine, he eloquently spoke out for the right-footers (the Catholics).

Hanged on a scaffold in Clonmel after a fabricated murder charge, his head severed and stuck on a spike over the Gaol of Clonmel that the birds never pecked, his executioner stoned to death at Philipstown near County Limerick.

'A shower of rain. You'll be drownded,' her father said as Kelsey left a bracelet of Turkish-blue slabs, each held to the other by double silver beads, on each slab an ikon – a grinning Padre Pio, the Blessed Virgin in various apparitions, recent popes – a child who treated herself to a sausage sandwich of Fridays and looked forward to it all week.

Grimalkin showers, fanatical showers, during which St Mary's Cathedral, built in the Great Famine years, same colour as the greyhounds that galloped on Bishops Meadows, looked like celluloid, town of barber shops and pubs, as many pubs as York they said.

'Do you know what my favourite animal is?' she'd say when he was a small boy and his grandfather, who'd dyed his hair blond, used carry him on the bar of his bicycle, 'Giraffes. I love giraffes,' and in Mick Tomo's Ruby Arts in York, the girl who frequently passed the car-cations on Dublin Port, got a tattoo of a giraffe wearing shades and afterwards walked on Little Hob Moor (Knavesmire), an ancient commons with hazel trees and dolphin schools of harebells – *méaracáin gorm* (blue thimbles), and saw the Plague Stone.

At York stone crosses, plague stones, vinegar stones were erected during an outbreak of plague in 1604 to denote temporary locations where trading could take place, each cross holding a small pool of water into which money could be placed and removed in trading.

Famine rain; where will we bury this Famine in us?

She'd left her son – a boy with eyes like a lost cache of thrush's eggs – in a town of Xtra-Vision and Argos streets but they are Famine streets, a framed relief model of the *Titanic* – Liverpool 1912 under it, Union Jack on its prow, with micro-photographs of its interior, of Captain Edward Smith, micro-*New York Times* front-page list of its dead – on permanent display in a shop window close to the advertisements of *007 Skyfall* and *Gears of War – The Judgment*, youths in combat outfits wheeling their babies as if they'd been shelled, strafed, torpedoed by these babies, through these Famine streets, walking their babies with the ferocious look of the men with mighty armalites against a burning city in the poster for *Gears of War – The Judgment*.

There are balloons from last night's Stag and Hen parties, blue, turquoise, green, orange on traffic posts, and a magenta ball in the shape of a rugby ball with 30 on it, suspended in the air by a woman who looks like a Humpty Dumpty that black hair had descended on, a squirrel's tail of hair at the back, with spectacular eyelash extensions.

Groups of youths stand in the rain that has begun to pour, discussing some recent fight, one of them – Dracula-hue to skin, scar over right eye, on crutches as a result of the combat, right leg in cast – licking the face of his mobile phone with the tip of his tongue, the others with smiles of schadenfreude at the injuries inflicted.

'It's the violence. Violence is the pleasure.'

Kelsey wandered past Bloomsbury Central Baptist Church muttering 'The Egyptian geese never pecked at Father Nicholas Sheehy's head,' thinking of the Egyptian geese breeding on Hampstead Heath, maybe having flown from Regent's Park – silver-green breasts, gold and green rumps, vermilion feet, beaks, cinnamon eyepatches.

I see the Penal Days in Naty's eyes.

'Why are people so fond of poker?'

'It's a bit of fun. Some play for pennies. Some for thousands. If you have a hundred thousand in the bank and don't know what to do with it. It takes their mind off the recession. They gamble and lose all they have. They lose all the time.'

Young Serbs play football on Sundays where Naty was mugged. Sometimes Croats. Some of the Croats mix with the Serbs. Some of them fight with one another.

Near The Pussycat Casino you see Serbian Santa Clauses. Black-and-white striped surcoats, white cuffs, black-and-white striped Phrygian hats, white petals on white beards.

'Was a sex shop first. Boys brought a girl there and had sex with her. Closed because it was corrupting youth.'

True to its provenance there's a sign outside with a lady in see-through underwear, transparent nylon stockings with white fastener bands, green eyeshadow, lipstick colour of the hearts, swinging her legs through a tear or hole in the Queen of Hearts.

'Off with their heads,' goes the Queen of Hearts in the children's stories and Amor, the Mauritian doorman with tattoo on his right leg of a polychromatic half moon with lasciviously grinning man's face-related this bit of history to Naty:

'The French came in 1917. Killed all the dodos and ate them. The dodos were like blue turkeys with hook beaks. They had no wings and they couldn't run away.

They killed all the giant turtles. Then the English came and killed all the French.'

Pochen, German 'to bluff.' Eighteenth-century Brag in England. From Pochen French developed Poque in New Orleans when Robert Emmet wearing a green-and-white uniform marched against Dublin Castle, the fiancée with whom he hid in Harold's Cross before he was captured and hung, herself leaving for Louisiana, the home of poker.

'She is far from the land where her young hero sleeps.'

'Oh breathe not the name.'

Medieval ancestral game Primero Spain. Primiera Italy. La Prime France.

English settlers in Louisiana anglicized it to Poker. Spread north along the Mississipi in riverboats and west during the Gold Rush.

Royal Flush (Flux). Full House. Wild card when, just before the Marquess of Queensbury rules were introduced, John L. Sullivan, who looked like a disgruntled Staffordshire terrier, defeated the walrus-moustached Paddy Ryan from Thurles, County Tipperary, in Mississippi City, near Gulfport, in bare-knuckle boxing.

'Poker you play against one another. Dice against the table. 21 (pontoon) against the dealer.

Double the deck, halve the winnings.

For 21 you need an ace and a ten.

Oxi, one of the fellows who plays at The Pussycat Casino, he works on the tracks – got an ace and a ten and other card tattoos on his fingers when he was a boy and they were badly done and he got them covered up. He had his name done on his other fingers and he had that covered up with skulls. He got Maori tattoos on his bald head. He has a horseshoe earring in one ear and a wooden stretcher in the other. They're African things.'

One for the road for this Scheherazade youth.

He used to bring tenners won at The Pussycat Casino or food from SuperValu or Dunnes Stores to a Traveller man who put on plastic gloves after bare-knuckle boxing and his eighteen-year-old son, who lived in the Wetlands.

'We're Travellers. Travellers live in a crowd,' a boy with freckles on face and forehead like beige dust raised by a horse's hooves, an azure in his eyes that had arrived on some sulky, said to him once as he crossed the greensward of a grey-crow-coloured estate.

Settled in a council house – a bull with a turf cut, ikonic chins, sleeper in each ear, tattoo of his name Padas on the back of his neck, chain bracelet thick as bacon-and-cabbage stew with black pudding and eggs in it.

His wife and other children had left him.

Sacred Heart wedding-gift picture on the wall.

Our Lady tree-stump replica on the mantelpiece – a seventy-year-old willow felled on the grounds of Holy Mary Parish Church in Rathkeale, County Limerick, was found to have created a stump with silhouette of Madonna and Child. Initially attacked with spray paint, later vandalized beyond recognition.

'Some people have nothing better to do,' said Padas.

Kush, eighteen-year-old son, would walk out naked at noon. Body suffering white with blotches like strawberry-and-cream sweets. Walked around. Then put on mouse-coloured trackie bottoms. Or boxers that made a statement – like ones with concentration-camp stripes or a pattern of playing cards.

Naty would go sulky racing in Troytown with them. In Polish wagon – shorter than the usual Dutch wagon, longer planks at the back, more room.

Drawn by a batty – skewbald – horse. Biscuit.

Sometimes by a snowflake-dapple blagdon mare with feathering (below the knee hair) – Midge (Medicine Woman). He took her out of Appleby where the Belfast escapade-ologist John Eagle, (name a shade different from the Dublin tattooist Johnny Eagle to whom army boys went for harps, daggers, tricolours), who bent six-inch nails, bars, horse shoes, extricated himself from mail bags until he was eighty.

'I was in Appleby three years running.' The Westmorland fells were blue, grey, green. Kush had seen in the windscreen mirror that the green of the Westmorland fells when they were receding was the same colour as his eyes.

The horse was a trotting horse picked up at Borris Horse Fair 15 August (Feast of the Assumption) a year earlier when Naty went with them. Black Beauty. Not called after a celebrity horse but after the Black Beauty roses that grew by the main street in Borris. Naty had worn a bow-tie the colour of those roses for his First Holy Communion, which his mother had not attended.

They swam Black Beauty in the Mountain River that comes down from Mount Leinster, where you can see the sixteen-arch viaduct, a bit shorter than the twenty-four-arch Ribblehead viaduct that Padas and Kush had seen on Batty Moor in Yorkshire, where the curlews sit on the stone walls as if they're sitting on thrones, on one of their trips to Appleby.

They returned to Kilkenny by Factory Cross, called after a coffin factory that was now just a derelict building, crossing Ballytiglea

Bridge from where you could see the horse line. Horses used pull the barges by the Barrow, sometimes through locks where the river was too rocky or where there were weirs.

During one of the famines that afflicted them, despite the snow-flake-dapple blagdon, despite Black Beauty, despite the Polish wagon, Padas and Kush went suddenly to London. Naty had a letter from Padas thanking him for the tenners, for the food from SuperValu and Dunnes Stores, and the food he had treated them to when they were downtown where there was the smell of fish and the sound of karaoke.

The Sacred-Heart picture found its way to one of Kilkenny's charity shops where a lady dwarf in a reflector jacket bought it.

'I am what I am.

I don't want to be what I am.

I hate being what I am.

They want you to be someone else. They boxed me twice on the head with a brick where I live. I live in the most dangerous part of Dublin.

They know everything about me.

Now they've given me drugs and I don't know what I am.'

A man with black-poodle hair, corpse-white chest with hair like the assassination-wastes of Coolock on it, was muttering to himself in his bed as Christmas light came to the hospital ward.

I am going to the operating theatre and Naty is getting a lift back to Kilkenny in an ambulance travelling to St Luke's General Hospital.

On the road on which he frequently travelled by Bus Éireann to Dublin.

Past Tiger Wash, Aldi, On the Run, Daybreak, Kia Motors (Home of the Seven Year Warranty), Goff Stud Farm since 1866.

Into Dublin City, past the signs screaming Online.

Online this, Online that, Online world, lost soul.

A Pentecostal slither of the Grand Canal and Legoland buildings, pylons, dispossessed emerald of fields.

'I'm going to a wedding in space,' Kelsey had said a few days before she died.

'Some people go to live in space,' Naty murmurs. 'They think a flying saucer will come and rescue them. Sometimes the flying saucer doesn't come.'

And as a black lady wheels in the breakfast trolley:

'How could anyone be that lonely?'

Kelsey had had a lavender umbrella with a duck's-head knob in her bag when she died.

On her mobile phone was a photograph of Naty, in scarlet tank top or racer, navy-blue-thongs, with triumphant upraised arm after a successful bout, a tortoiseshell butterfly in the ring, eyes the blue of a statue of Mary from an Irish Industrial School.

'Back for the big gamble in The Pussycat Casino on Sunday night.'

'I often go walking in Kilkenny town.'

'I'll give you a shout if I see you.'

It is August the fifteenth – Borris Horse Fair day – and Naty, Padas and Kush are returning over the Ballytiglea – Bally-Tadhg-lea – Bridge in a Polish wagon.

Horses would tow the barges up and down under the bridge, where the loosestrife blooms now, scarlet lords and ladies, cuckoo-pint (cuckoo-penis) in the hedges that lead to the river.

Grain was carried upriver from the tidal estuary where Polish youths open tins of Sweet Harvest sweetcorn to lure the dace, the thwaite shad, the giant sea lampreys in, to upstream brewers.

Pigs, turf, beet, coal, beer in barrels (publicans bottled it themselves) downstream.

There are still winches by the river, lost among the rosebay willowherb, the meadowsweet, the Himalayan balsam, the bush vetch, the brambles, which helped the horses pull their loads, mile markers, boulders that they used tie the barges to.

Locks were named after the people who owned the land they were on, Nolan's Lock, Gorman's Lock.

East and West they called the two sides of the river and most of the barge men were from the West side.

The towns, like Athy where Julie Mahon used ride a high nelly in a safari hat and gabardene coat winter and summer, never married, pitched the turf herself, and where there is the One Horse Bridge over the Barrow, just wide enough for a bargeman to lead a horse from the Grand Canal towpath to the Barrow towpath, had oats and hay stores and bunk beds for the bargeman. The journey from where the tidal estuary begins at the monastic ruins of St Mullins – St Mullin (St Molig) was able to walk on the Barrow and he built a canal himself that became a place of pilgrimage – took two days and one night to Dublin.

Ballytiglea Bridge with its rusticated (roughened surface) arch stones and triangular cutwaters (pier projections) was built around the time of the Kilkenny river floods of 1763 (Thomastown Bridge, proximate to St Nicholas's legendary burial place, was swept away). It appeared on Scotsmen George Taylor's and Andrew Skinner's revised map of 1783 (first edition 1778, price one guinea). After indicating the big houses and bridges of Ireland they went to the American wars where Lord Edward Fitzgerald was fighting and mapped there.

On their Irish map distances were in both Irish miles and English miles.

An Irish mile is always longer, harder, more obdurate.

Irish miles have known the Penal Days, another language, have been traipsed to market towns and immemorial fairs.

'Two blanks. Blank like my wife. One winning one. Find the King. King of Hearts. King of Diamonds. If you don't court you'll never marry,' the Three-card-trick man, his arms covered in Johnny Eagle tattoos (dwarf pirate with huge pirate hat, Death rather than Dishonour, flask shape with the names of his nine sisters in it) went at the Borris Fair.

Children fired bi-coloured BB guns; the small walrussy man in clown's tartan who locks himself in a cubicle in the toilet of Kilkenny railway station and soliloquys to himself was there (everyone is at home at the Borris Horse Fair); wreaths made of silk flowers and florist's ribbon (crosses, electric guitars, horses' heads, pillows) were sold; tiger-head throws; Burberry caps; pictures of Our Lady appearing to Lúcia, Jacinta, Francisco with cracks at the sides; raffle tickets for a draw to purchase one and one-quarter acres of land to extend Ballymurphy Cemetery (near the place where Father John Murphy who learnt Latin and Greek from a hedge-school master, studied theology in Seville, in flight with his horse's shoes turned the wrong way so the enemy couldn't trace him, said his last Mass in the stable in which he'd slept on 29 June 1798, the Feast of Saints Peter and Paul, put his blessing on the place and because of that sick cattle brought there thereafter and cured); pictures of Joe Bugner who with his intense embrosse hair, very fine lips, reddish complexion, looks like an Irish Traveller ('He fought with Mohammed Ali twice and he didn't win. He should have won'); MCing, fast talk tapes, Traveller youths affecting a Southern hip-hop accent and recording themselves. 'I'm coming Home.'

Padas went to Appleby after coming home from Mountjoy. Five years. Bucket for a toilet.

'It's the heart,' Padas is saying, 'Ireland is where the heart is.

I come from a family of twenty-two if they were all still living. Eight sisters. Eleven brothers. Living on the side of the road.

I left school at twelve. I had to. I wouldn't do that to Kush. I'd let him go as far as he can.

Ma was mad about her sons. She said you must always stick together in tragedy.

A week after my mother died I was in Athlone by the Shannon, the centre of Ireland, visiting the Hartys at a halting site and the shades handcuffed me and took me to the shade camp and beat me up. They wouldn't let me see a doctor. I had to get fifteen stitches. They did everything to spite me.

I go back and forwards. I had a passport but I lost it.

I have an aunt in Preston with twenty-four sons and a daughter. I have an uncle in Newcastle but it's too far away, and a cousin in Oxford.

He's banned because he was blackguarding the steering wheel and drove ten days later and got six years.

There's a river in Milton Keynes called the Ouze and my brother and I went for a swim in it on a hot day. He was dragged down by the wormwood.'

Yellow water-lilies on the Barrow now under a cirrus sky.

'I had another brother of nineteen, he was as wild as a ram. Used to lose his trousers running away, it would fall to his ankles:

Three of them escaped without a scratch. His head went through the window. He was killed. God rest him.

They kicked the poor over there. Many of them had to leave.

Ireland is where the heart is.

Kush is making me ould. I'll be a grandfather before I know. I'll need a walking stick. No, I'm still young. I'm still a pup. You're not a pup for long. The young fellows are passing me out.'

The militia blew up the eastern side of the dreamy seven-arch Graigue Bridge – Cistercians had come from Wiltshire to build the abbey by the bridge in the thirteenth century, already attempt made to mend it – and Father John Murphy and Miles Byrne – seventeen years old that year when he was made head of the Wexford pikemen – and their men couldn't cross it.

They didn't cross at Ballytiglea Bridge but at the nine-arch Goresbridge with its smoothly finished arch stones and walls made of Mount Leinster rubble instead.

Goresbridge was built in 1756 by Sir Robert Gore who had a horse with two names, Black and All Black, and Othello, and a few years before Goresbridge was built it raced against a horse called Bazajet, owned by the Earl of March, at the Curragh.

Bazajet's rider dropped his saddle cloth or weight cloth during the race that Black or All Black won anyway – a cloth with flat lead pieces worn when the jockey's weight is less than the horse must carry.

It was returned to him at the weighing out and Sir Robert spotted this and called a duel.

When the Earl of March turned up with pistols for the duel next day there was a coffin with his name and date of death.

He quickly apologized.

Despite the nine-arch bridge the Gore family got into debt and the last member left for America about the time Miles Byrne left Ireland in a Yankee vessel, bound for Lisbon, captained by Captain O'Connor from Wexford, now a United Stats citizen, getting as far as the mouth of the Gironde with it.

Father Murphy and Miles Byrne captured Goresbridge, defeated the Fourth Dragoon Guards and the Wexford Militia, took prisoners, found an abundance of flour, marched up the bogcotton Mount Leinster where they lit Midsummer fires, slaughtered sheep, the women following the men making bread, the wounded dressed in linen bandages soaked in whiskey, and in the night when the rebels slept a terrible thing happened, some of the Wexford Militia prisoners, Catholics, persecuted by their fellow soldiers and threatened with death because of suspected United Irishman leanings, murdered their persecutors.

Miles Byrne chose a black servant prisoner in livery to stand on the Big Bridge (it's a small bridge) over the Deen at Castlecomer with a white handkerchief tied to a cane above his head to stop English fire from the house of Lady Anne Butler.

And Padas talks of another war:

'They built the bridges in Germany during the war naked. They didn't have the time to put on clothes. Their clothes were blown off. It's a wonder they lost the war.'

And then:

'A sheik and Moslems came to Goresbridge to buy horses and they asked for a place to pray.

They had a look at the Church of the Holy Trinity and St George of Grange Sylvae and they didn't want to pray in them.

They went to the house of the man they were buying horses from to pray.

If you went to Dubai would you ask for a place to pray?'

Acknowledgments

The Big River
Southword, June 2008
Editor: Nuala Ni Chonchuir
American Short Fiction, Spring 2009
Editor: Stacey Swann

Café Remember
Princeton University Library Chronicle,
Autumn 2010
Editor: Gretchen M. Oberfranc

From the Town
The White Review, 2011
Editors: Benjamin Eastman and
Jacques Testard

The History of Magpies
Cyphers, Spring 2010
Editors: Leland Bardwell, Eiléan Ní
Chuilleanáin, Pearse Hutchinson,
Macdara Woods
The Clifden Anthology, 2012
Editor: Brendan Flynn

Kennedy
The Stinging Fly, Summer 2010
Editor: Sean O'Reilly
Best European Fiction 2012, Dalkey
Archive Press
Editor: Aleksander Hemon

Wooden Horse
The Stinging Fly, Summer 2012
Editor: Dave Lordan
The House of Mourning and Other Stories,
Dalkey Archive Press, 2013

Brimstone Butterfly
Town and Country, New Irish Short
Stories 2013
Faber and Faber, Editor: Kevin Barry

Thornback Ray
Gorse, January 2014
Editors: Susan Tomaselli and
David Gavan

The Spindle Tree
Town Stitched by River, Dublin
UNESCO City of Literature
International Writing Program at
the University of Iowa, Iowa City,
UNESCO City of Literature 2015
Editors: Alan Hayes and
Christopher Merrill

The Metlar
Winter Pages, Curlew Editions, 2015
Editors: Kevin Barry and
Olivia Smith

Walking through Truth Land
The Stinging Fly, Spring 2016
Editor: Sean O'Reilly

Famine Rain
Cyphers, Spring 2017
Editors: Eiléan Ní Chuilleanáin
and Macdara Woods